Jacques Poulin

MISTER BLUE

Translated from the French by Sheila Fischman

archipelago books

Archipelago Books
232 3rd Street #A111
Brooklyn, NY 11215
www.archipelagobooks.org

Library of Congress Cataloging-in-Publication Data
Poulin, Jacques, 1937-
[Vieux chagrin. English]
Mister Blue / by Jacques Poulin ; translated from the French by Sheila Fischman.
– 1st Archipelago Books ed.
p. cm.
ISBN 978-1-935744-31-3 (pbk.)
1. Novelists – Fiction 2. Cats – Fiction. I. Fischman, Sheila. II. Title.
PQ3919.2.P59V5413 2011
843'.914–dc22   2011023704

Distributed by Consortium Book Sales and Distribution
www.cbsd.com

Cover: Detail from *Portrait de Franz Pforr* by Johann Friedrich Overbeck, 1810
The publication of *Mister Blue* was made possible with support from
Lannan Foundation, the National Endowment for the Arts, and the
New York State Council on the Arts, a state agency.

CONTENTS

CONVERSATION

(amiably, standing on the doorstep)

How are things on earth?
– Fine, fine, very fine.
Are the little dogs flourishing?
– Oh my goodness yes, indeed they are.
What about the clouds?
– Drifting.
And the volcanoes?
– Simmering.
And the rivers?
  Floating.
Time?
– Unwinding.
And your soul?
– Sick
    the springtime was too green
    my soul ate too much salad.

JEAN TARDIEU, *The Hidden River*

MISTER BLUE

FOOTPRINTS

Spring had arrived.

The day was so mild that I came down from the attic earlier than usual. I went out on the beach with Mr. Blue and walked to the end of the bay. I was taking a little rest, sitting on a rock that faced the river, when suddenly I noticed some footprints in the sand.

Out of curiosity, I placed my own foot in one of the prints. I was surprised to observe that they were exactly the same size. And yet these were not my prints: I hadn't walked here for several days, and there had been time for the tide, which was very high, to obliterate my trail.

Mr. Blue was just as intrigued as I was. With his tail in the air like a question mark and his muzzle in the sand, the old cat sniffed at the prints. They led directly to a little cave I already knew was there, which one entered by edging through a very narrow gap.

The cave was divided into two rooms. In the larger one, which must have been four meters wide and three meters high, I found the remains of a campfire. Mr. Blue, who got there before me, was nosing among the remains of a fire in the middle of the floor. On a sort of long, narrow shelf formed by a projection of the rock face sat a candle, a book, and a box of matches.

I went closer to look at the book: it was *The Arabian Nights*. I would have liked to pick it up and turn the pages, but something held me back. I had the feeling that to do so would be indiscreet. It was as if I were in some person's bedroom. I mean: in everything I could see there – the footprints, the objects, even in the air itself – there was a sense of somebody's soul. I didn't touch the book. I didn't touch anything, I didn't even visit the second room in the cave; I went back to the house.

I lived in an old frame house that stood all alone in the middle of the bay. It looked rather odd because it had been built in stages. Originally, it had been a simple cottage that my father had gradually transformed, adding a bedroom, a shed, and a second floor, as the family grew. The resulting house was a hodgepodge that boasted a number of styles and was topped by a number of roofs, whose slopes intersected. The weight of the snow and ice that accumulated there during the winter had weakened the roofing, making it susceptible to bad weather, and during severe summer storms, the rain would sometimes drip into the attic and leak into one of the bedrooms upstairs.

After several years in Europe, I now almost always spent my summers in the old house. Every year, it became a little more dilapidated: it was falling into ruin faster than I could repair it. It was my childhood home. Many years before, it had been part of the village of Cap-Rouge. Then my father had it moved into the bay where there were no other people because he wanted peace and quiet. It had been loaded onto a flat-bottomed boat that was half raft and half barge, transported across the river, and set down in the middle of the bay. My father and some other men had stood on the beach, watching the house move along the river. As I remember it, I was on the boat myself, but perhaps that's something I've imagined, because I was very young at the time.

When I walked into the kitchen, I glanced, as usual, at the big electric Coca-Cola clock. It indicated a few minutes past noon. I fed the cat his fish, then I had a soft-boiled egg with toast, mild cheese, and a little honey. The house was huge: there were three stories and five bedrooms, but it was in the attic that I felt most at ease for working. Because of a nagging back problem, I wrote standing up, facing a dormer window that looked out on the river. I would place my writing pad on a breadbox that sat on a desk. (The breadbox came just to my elbows and it provided a convenient storage place for pens and paper.) When the words wouldn't come, I walked, pacing the attic.

That afternoon, I paced for longer than usual, but I was making very little progress in my work. I couldn't take my mind off the book I'd seen in the cave, and I still had the feeling that I'd been indiscreet, that I'd even violated someone's privacy. Finally, I came down from the attic and went out to sit on the sun porch.

The sun porch on the second floor was my favorite room in the old house. It was long and narrow, with a dozen windows. Sunlight flooded it during the day and there was no better place to read, especially in the spring and the fall. The chairs were comfortable and you could rest your feet on the window ledge in front of you. There was a small bookcase at either end and, in one corner, a walnut writing desk that held papers and an old photograph album.

MARIKA

I was unable to write the way I wanted, either that day or the next. After two days, I decided to go back to the cave. Though it was only six p.m., the sun was sinking: in late April, the days are still not very long.

To keep Mr. Blue from coming with me, I gave him a big dish of cat food; I wanted to be alone. I took a flashlight and went out on the beach. The cave was on my right, at the very end of the bay, near a little sandy inlet. From the house to the inlet was no more than two kilometers, but just when you thought you'd arrived, you still had to cross a stretch of rocky scree that had fallen from the cliff and now extended to the middle of the sandbar.

Once past the scree, I started humming a tune to announce my arrival to anyone who might be in the cave. I hummed a song by Brassens, "Il n'y a pas d'amour heureux." Whenever I feel like humming,

I don't know why but that old song is the one that always comes to mind. As I approached the cave, to make even more noise, I pretended to be looking for old Mr. Blue and I called him several times in a loud voice. I pricked up my ears and, hearing nothing, I went in, edging through the narrow gap.

There was no one inside, either in the big room or the small one, but I saw right away that *The Arabian Nights* had been moved. Even though I felt again that I was being indiscreet, that I was interfering in somebody's private life, this time I picked up the book. With a slight pang, I slowly turned the pages. On the flyleaf a name and an initial were written in blue ink: Marie K. I said it under my breath and from that moment, in my head and in my heart, the name "Marika" would reverberate forever.

A WELCOME NOTE

The book that I was writing in the attic, every day except Saturday and Sunday, was a love story. But I was having trouble defining the female character and my progress was very slow.

I paced, I looked out the window, I pondered anything at all, even old tennis matches I'd argued about with my brother. And, of course, I thought about Marika. One day when I couldn't work in any case, I decided to write to her. I went back to the kitchen to make myself a coffee, and on my way back to the attic, the words came rushing all together in my head, and almost in one go I wrote her this brief note:

Dear Marika,

Welcome. Old Mr. Blue and I hope your visit here will be a pleasant one, as much as our inhospitable shores allow. Try not to let the cold and the damp bother you too much. Walk on the beach and the sandbar as much as you want: that's an excellent way to shake off your worries, as I've often discovered for myself.

I have lived alone for a long time and solitude is propitious for my work, but it warms my heart to know that you're at the other end of the bay. Now that you're there, everything seems possible, even the wildest, most secret dreams, the ones we never talk about, those that lurk beneath the surface of ourselves. I cannot help thinking that your presence is a kind of invitation to begin everything again, to start from scratch.

Though I don't yet know your face, you already live in my heart.

I reread the letter. Its inappropriate and overwrought tone irritated me, so I decided to keep it for myself and use it later in the story I was writing.

THE OAK WITHOUT
A HEART

Every spring, I had an urgent need to see colors, and that year I was very lucky. Along with the opening of the first leaves, which were a very tender green, there arrived not only the snow geese and the Canada geese, but also flocks of grosbeaks that scattered shifting patches of black and yellow all around, as well as blackbirds, juncos, and several house finches; I spotted some swallows too, and even a pair of blackburnian warblers.

In early May, persistent heavy rain had finished off the last pile of snow that still stood between the shed and the cliff. The wind turned westerly, the temperature rose, and since I didn't want to miss the opening of the first buds, I started keeping an eye on the four young birches huddled together in front of the house. There were a lot of trees around the old house: oaks, maples, a service tree, and several varieties of conifers, but birches have always been the ones I like best.

The oaks were most numerous, however. They were old and there was something special about them all. One of them, which I called "the oak without a heart," was lower than the others and appeared fairly sound if you looked at it through a window; but if you approached it from the beach, you could see that it was ripped open from top to bottom and that the trunk was hollow: the old oak tree didn't have a heart. Nevertheless, it was in no worse shape than the other oaks, which were all weakened by age to some extent. There were some dead branches, of course, but at the height of summer the old oak's foliage was just as dense as that of its neighbors.

At the base of another oak, the one nearest the house, there was a hole five or six centimeters across – through which, one fine morning, I spied first the pointed muzzle and then the striped back of a chipmunk. Later on, I saw the whole family: an adult (most likely the mother) and three little ones.

Before venturing outside their burrows, the chipmunks waited till the grass was fairly high. They must have been looking out for cats. In fact, all sorts of stray cats prowled the neighborhood, especially when the moon was full. They were very brazen and sometimes went inside the house, entering through a hole in the screen of a small basement window. They would take up residence in the cellar or the shed, and they'd even go to the kitchen and tuck into old Mr. Blue's cat food. Then one day they left the way they'd come, and I didn't know if I would see them again. All cats were my friends. I had a preference for those that came back every summer: there was Charade, who was more or less Siamese, deaf, and had one brown eye and one blue one; Vitamin, a white cat who often had kittens; and Samurai, a pugnacious big yellow tom who was always growling.

To my great sorrow, the cats seemed to take a vicious pleasure in persecuting squirrels and chipmunks. They'd light into all varieties of squirrels – the gray ones, the red ones, the black – but their favorite target was quite obviously the family of little chipmunks that lives at the foot of the oak tree nearest the house.

It was the mother chipmunk who was always the first one to stick her muzzle outside the burrow, then venture outside; a moment later, the three youngsters would follow suit. While the little ones looked for food around the oak, the mother, standing on her hind legs so she could see over the tall grass, would nervously turn her head this way and that, ready to sound the alarm at the slightest sound of danger. She had to be particularly wary of Vitamin, because the white cat's hunting instincts were highly developed, and she often hid close by, in the hollow trunk of the "oak without a heart."

DINARZADE

As often as my back allowed me (it was still weak following a lumbar sprain), I played tennis with my younger brother, Francis.

I have a long-standing love affair with tennis that began when I was just a child and the house hadn't yet made its journey down the river. Tennis was the sole activity at which, despite the effects of age, I was still making some progress. In my work as a writer, my love life – my life, period – I had achieved only moderate success, or, in any case, far inferior to what I'd hoped for when I was young.

When I played tennis, something astonishing occurred now and then, something I couldn't explain: it was as if my body and my soul suddenly found themselves in perfect harmony. During the few precious minutes that this harmony lasted, I was able to effortlessly execute shots that considerably surpassed my usual game; I barely felt the impact of the ball on my racket, so well coordinated were my movements. To my brother, who was amazed at this sudden success, I would laugh and say that I was playing with Martina Navratilova's racket, and that every now and then, she'd lean over my shoulder to help me out.

Coming home after a match at noon one Saturday, I had just parked the Volkswagen minibus at the top of the cliff and I was about to descend the steep path to the house, my tennis bag slung over my shoulder, when I caught sight of a little sailboat off the sandy inlet. At that distance you couldn't see very clearly, but it seemed to me that the sailboat was riding at anchor.

I wolfed down my soup and sandwich, rested for a moment on the sun porch while I leafed through the weekend papers, then rushed out to see what was going on at the sandy inlet. As I was coming in sight of the sailboat, just beyond the scree, I could hear sawing and hammering. The sailboat, to which a small skiff was moored, was about eight meters long and in not very good shape: it listed to one side, the hull was battered, and part of the cabin seemed rotten. The only thing about it that looked new was the name, freshly painted in blue, which I could read on the hull: *Dinarzade*.

The name, which was that of Scheherazade's sister, reassured me. In all likelihood it indicated that the boat was Marika's and that she had moved into the cave while she was repairing it. Besides, by listening closely to the sound of the tools, I could tell there was only one person working on the boat, and so I drew the obvious conclusion: Marika was alone.

THE SLOWEST WRITER
IN QUEBEC

Around nine o'clock the following Monday morning, when I went up to the attic to write, the first thing I did after I'd set my cup of coffee on the desk was to open the dormer window so I could lean out and look to the right. I was glad to see the sailboat was still there.

I took my manuscript and pen from the breadbox and reread the chapter I'd abandoned the Friday before. My hero was in a bar in Old Quebec. He was drinking a Tia Maria while he sat at a corner table listening to a song the bartender had put on the record player. It was "Lili Marlene," an old song my character was very fond of, and Marlene Dietrich was singing. He was looking nostalgically at the cigarette smoke that rose in bluish scrolls toward the ceiling. He was also looking at the back of a girl who was seated at the bar. When the song had ended, she was going to turn toward him – at least that's what I had imagined – and then he would finally see her face.

For the time being, he was letting himself be lulled by the song, which was in German. He didn't understand the lyrics except for the odd word that sounded like "lamppost" and "barracks," but it was obviously a song about love, for the rather harsh voice was warm and caressing, and he felt almost as cozy as if Marlene had wrapped her arms around his shoulders.

Slowly, the music died away. The bartender closed the cover of the record player, as if "Lili Marlene" were the very last song to be heard here below, and my hero's eyes were still riveted on the back of the girl who was sitting with her elbows on the bar. He was waiting for her to turn around, and I waited with him. We were two different people, he and I. There was a resemblance, but he was ten years younger, he could have been my younger brother.

The girl didn't turn around. I capped my pen and, as usual, began pacing the attic. I wasn't impatient, I wasn't even concerned. One had to wait and let things ripen. Of course I, as the author, could intervene, but interventions of that kind – I knew from experience – detracted from the story's authenticity. I don't want to suggest, though, that I'd given the matter a great deal of thought. In fact, all I knew about the art of writing I'd picked up from interviews with Ernest Hemingway, which I'd actually read before I myself was a writer: at the time I'd been a professor, a Hemingway specialist.

Far from being an author who thought a great deal, I was one who allowed instinct or intuition to be my guide. The trouble with such a method was that the work advanced very slowly. After an hour and a half in that bar in Old Quebec, my characters still hadn't moved, the record player was still silent, and the entire scene was frozen in absolute immobility.

The man who was pacing the attic was, beyond any doubt, the slowest writer in Quebec.

PAPA HEMINGWAY

As the words were taking their time, I let anxiety and doubt gradually steal over me and I even began to question the worth of my subject. Was trying to write a love story such a good idea? While I was pacing up and down, turning the question over and over in my mind, I suddenly remembered that Hemingway had something to say on the subject. And if memory served me right, it was in one of the famous interviews. I went over to my bedroom on the main floor to look in the leather chest with ornamental gilt hinges where I kept old lecture notes, manuscripts, and various papers. At least fifteen years had passed since I'd stopped teaching, but it didn't take me too long to lay my hands on the interview. I found it in one of my favorite books, *Papa Hemingway*, by A. E. Hotchner. In the passage I was looking for, old Hemingway set forth a very simple rule: a writer must stick to the subject he knows best.

I had to acknowledge that I'd broken this rule. I was trying to write a love story without being in love myself. I'd probably chosen this subject because, as I felt myself growing older, I was afraid it was too late to fall in love one last time.

There were two ways out of the impasse: either change my subject, or take a closer interest in that person named Marika. I chose the second solution.

As I was hesitant by nature, this decision was made only after a period of hemming and hawing and changing my mind that went on for several days. Besides, instead of trying to find a way to put my decision into practice, I allowed myself to daydream, and wasted time wondering what Hemingway would have done if it had been he who had seen the footprints in the sand.

First of all, by looking at the prints he would have guessed some things about the person who had arrived through the sandy inlet. He certainly would have been able to tell the person's sex, age, character, or mood: reading tracks was an art he had learned from the Indians with whom he'd fished and hunted in Michigan during his youth.

After that he would definitely have tried to perform some feat to impress Marika: he was always trying to impress people. He'd have sailed up on his yacht, the *Pilar*; he'd have dropped anchor into the open water, and swum to her with just one arm while holding a bottle of champagne and glasses aloft with the other, and with his clothes bundled up and attached to his head with his belt.

But if she hadn't been there, he'd have been philosophical about it. He'd have gone back to his yacht and, after loading a rowboat with provisions (bread, wine, cheese, and ham), his sleeping bag, camping gear, and something to read, he'd have rowed back to shore, made himself comfortable, and waited.

When he saw her coming back, barefoot, from a walk along the beach, he'd have offered her a glass of champagne, saying: "It's not as cold as it would be at Harry's Bar in Venice, dear lady, but I thought a glass of this excellent Mumm's was the only thing worthy of celebrating our first meeting." Old Hemingway would have spoken with a false humility that was utterly convincing.

He would have asked how she had sorted out her problem with the sailboat; she would have told him about the repairs, and he'd have nodded knowingly. In return, she would ask a question about his yacht, and he'd leap at the chance to tell her all about the *Pilar*, explaining how, during the Second World War, it had been a fishing boat rigged for hunting German submarines; he'd have told her about the letter from the Secretary of Defense or something like that congratulating the crew on their bravery during the hostilities.

Finally, she'd have invited him into the cave for something hot to drink and he'd have accepted eagerly. He would have examined her setup with a connoisseur's eye and praised her efforts to battle the humidity. Then, spying her copy of *The Arabian Nights,* he would have pointed to the notice on the title page: "Traduction par Antoine Galland." And he'd have told her when it was that the translator had made his three journeys to the Near East and given her the publication dates for the twelve volumes of the first edition. And he would have explained, citing precise examples, how Antoine Galland had transformed the original Arabic tales, deleting or even inventing passages to make them conform to the tastes of eighteenth-century readers in France. She would have been amazed at the extent to which old Hemingway – tough guy and big game hunter – had a detailed and wide-ranging knowledge of literature.

Soon, he'd have got up to leave. He would have clasped her hand, bowing slightly, and apologized for having disturbed her, and then perhaps she would have seen a little glimmer of sadness in his eyes, but just for a second. Her memory of him would be that of an amiable man who was full of life and full of warmth.

IF I WERE YOU

I don't know if old Hemingway managed to pass on to me some of his legendary courage, but the following Saturday I composed an invitation to Marika, this time with the firm intention of taking it to her in the cave.

The letter was longer than I'd intended and it read as follows:

Dear Stranger,

If I were you, one of these evenings I'd make my way toward the old frame house that sits at the end of the bay. Your visit would be much appreciated.

In the event that you're bashful, please know that you have nothing to fear from the man who lives in the house: though he's a little peculiar, like anyone who has lived alone for a long time, he's not dangerous;

he is a maniac, but only about words. His sole companion is an old cat called Mr. Blue. He spends all day writing in the attic. Actually, he doesn't look as if he's working: he walks, he paces, he stops at the dormer window and gazes out at the river. His head is full of words that swarm in there as in a beehive; sometimes the hive is empty.

What does he look like? He's a skinny man and his face is gaunt. If he had on a red knitted cap, he would look like Commander Cousteau's brother. And his hair is going gray.

Ever since he first saw your footprints in the sand, he's been thinking about you a lot and now he can't write. He walks even more than usual, seeking in vain the proper words, the appropriate turns of phrase. And in the evening when his work is done and he has eaten and walked on the beach for a while, he goes to the sun porch, where he likes to sit for hours watching the moon shimmer on the water and the lights of the city across the river sparkle in the night, telling people it's all right now to give themselves over to their daydreams and to the melancholy of their memories.

I didn't like the last lines very much.

Words are independent, like cats, and they don't do what you want them to do. You can love them, stroke them, say sweet things to them all you want – they still break off and go their own way. Toward the end of the letter, they had slipped away between my fingers.

But I wasn't going to turn it into a tragedy. Time was passing and I wanted to stop dawdling and go to the cave. I wanted very much to see Marika and find out if she was really alone.

At the bottom of the page I wrote just my first name, Jim, then I slipped the invitation into an envelope and went out to the beach. Mr. Blue wasn't there. After a while, when I turned to see if he was following me, I spotted him in the distance on the sandbar; he'd climbed onto a big rock and I thought I saw the slender shape of Vitamin beside him.

On the other side of the scree, I noticed that while the sailboat was in its usual place, the little skiff wasn't there. And this time there was no sound from the sailboat: all I heard was the plaintive cry of the gulls, the lapping of the rising tide, and the distant rumble of traffic along the two bridges that straddled the river.

When I got to the sandy inlet, I saw that the skiff was moored to a stake on the beach, just across the cave, and my heart started thumping wildly. I stood for a moment rooted to the spot, then I turned and raced back to the scree. And there I sat on the ground amid the rocks and tried to regain my calm.

I was ashamed of running away like a coward. On the contrary, I wasn't fearful and I wasn't a loser, not even a beautiful loser. I was quite simply a Libra, a goddamn Libra, in other words, a divided man, torn between contradictory wishes. My dithering, which was nothing new and which I loathed with all my heart, didn't really surprise me. What did surprise me – a lot – was the profound turmoil in which the mere presence of a woman whom I hadn't even seen had thrown me.

I started mulling things over. Marika was in the cave and all I had to do, in fact, was approach it, making a little noise as I'd done the other day, or asking aloud: "Anybody home?" The rest would come by itself:

either I would tell her who I was and what I wanted, or else I'd simply hand her the invitation and go away, after wishing her a good day.

Filled with new resolve, I rose and headed directly for the sandy inlet. The nearby sound of an animal scurrying across the gravel startled me: it was old Mr. Blue, who was very enthusiastically chasing Vitamin. This wink of fate (at least that was how I interpreted it) encouraged me, even though it was rather belated. Twenty paces from the cave, I made as much noise as I could by kicking at the stones and chunks of wood, then I asked twice if anyone was home. No answer came. I hesitated very briefly, looked all around, and then, holding my envelope, slipped into the cave.

My edginess disappeared all at once. No one was there. I felt a peculiar mixture of emotions: disappointment, but at the same time, relief. And I still had one small concern: Marika had gone out onto the beach, probably to gather wood, and she would come back at any moment. I stepped forward to take a look inside the smaller room and saw that it served as a bedroom because there was a sleeping bag, an oil lamp, and a leather bag that looked like a toilet kit.

Her book, *The Arabian Nights*, was still on the rocky shelf. When I opened it again for the pleasure of seeing the name on the flyleaf, Marie K., I saw at once that the fringed bookmark had been moved: it now marked the page where began the tale of the twenty-second night, entitled "Tale of the Ensorcelled Prince, Lord of the Black Islands." My attention was drawn to this curious phrase: "He was a man only from his head to his waist [. . .] and the other half of his body was black marble." I didn't have a lot of time for reflection, so I left my invitation in a conspicuous place near the book. Before I left, I looked all over for signs of another person's presence, but there were none.

Back at the house, Mr. Blue was waiting for me on the front steps and I thought I detected something superior, even ironic, in the way he was looking at me.

BUNGALOW

The kitchen was messy and grimy.

I washed the dishes that were sitting in the sink, I swept and vacuumed (the old Electrolux made a terrible racket), I even scrubbed the wooden floor. Then, as I was looking out the window to see if Marika was coming, I realized that the panes were dirty, so I hastened to clean them with Windex, inside and out.

I opened the cupboard for the third or fourth time to check that the bottles of Scotch, Cinzano, and Saint-Raphaël were there, along with several bottles of wine, and that I had freshly ground coffee as well as an assortment of tea, both black and herbal.

Everything was ready.

Now I just had to wait.

I went upstairs to get a book from the sun porch. Novels were at one end of the room, practical books at the other. I looked at the novels, trying to decide which one to choose, and when I couldn't make up my mind, I began stroking their spines. That's an old trick: if you stroke the spines of books gently with the palm of your hand, you can sometimes feel vibrations or a kind of warmth. This time, though, I was too worked up, and I didn't feel a thing, so I took the first book that came to hand. It was a novel by Colette, *Chéri*. Just as I was taking it from the shelf, a clear, sharp image from the past came to me, like a flashback in a movie, and I chased it immediately from my mind: a woman, still young, who was going to go away with another man, was removing her books from a bookcase, leaving shelves filled with blank spaces like gaps in a brick wall.

I took Colette's novel down to the kitchen. To read it, I leaned on the counter opposite the window that looks out on the beach: I had only to look up to see if anyone was coming.

Even though they were very different writers, I enjoyed reading Colette just as much as Hemingway. Whenever I read her, I'm amazed at how precisely she describes sounds, smells, colors, everything in nature. That evening, though, I wasn't really reading: I kept looking out the window, turning pages rather absentmindedly, while the book took me to Neuilly and to Paris, down the *allées* in the Bois de Boulogne. Then I strolled along the *grands boulevards*, stopping for a *café crème* . . . and I don't know how long I had been sitting there on the terrace of a café when a sickening smell brought me abruptly back to reality.

Old Mr. Blue was rubbing against my legs and it was quite obvious that he was the source of the stench. His paws were covered with mud and he had left his prints all over the kitchen floor that I'd just washed. I looked out the window: a fine rain was falling.

The electric Coca-Cola clock showed seven-forty and I was starting to think that Marika wouldn't turn up. I fed Mr. Blue some chicken, then got down on my hands and knees to wipe up his muddy paw prints with a damp cloth. When I got close to him, I realized why he smelled so bad: he'd been outside spraying to mark his territory.

I was rinsing my cloth in the sink and looking out abstractedly at the rain, when suddenly I saw someone walking along the beach. The person was wearing a bright yellow vinyl raincoat with a hood and was heading straight for the house!

I rushed to the bathroom. I took the can of Florient off the toilet tank, stood in the kitchen doorway and gave Mr. Blue a long lavender-scented spray, then I aimed four shorter ones at the four corners of the room. The old cat sped to the cellar stairs. I put the can back and quickly seated myself at the kitchen table. I pretended to be reading the newspaper; it was a week old, but I made as if I were engrossed in the news.

My heart was pounding tumultuously.

I took a deep breath and when I heard a knock at the door, I said: "Come in!" as naturally as I could. I acted as if nothing special was going on. As if women were always dropping anchor off the cove and coming to my house for a drink.

The woman in the yellow raincoat pushed open the door.

Doing my best to appear calm, I slowly raised my head to see what she looked like. She was a big, broad-shouldered woman, maybe forty years old. She had on jeans and black rubber boots like the kind you wear to go fishing. Water dripped from her raincoat onto the oval braided rug where she was standing. She wiped her feet and looked around the kitchen.

"Smells good in here!" she said with a touch of irony.

I couldn't think of anything to say. Fortunately, old Mr. Blue was coming up from the cellar. He was thirsty and I got up to give him some milk. The woman shed her yellow raincoat and dropped it onto the braided rug beside her boots.

"Are you expecting someone?" she asked.

"Yes," I said. "Marika . . ."

"That's not me," she said. "My name's Bungalow."

She went over to Mr. Blue and petted him while he lapped up his milk.

"That's not my real name," she said. "It's what the girls call me."

"The girls?"

"Right, you don't know the girls. There's a group of us, we bought a house in Old Quebec and fixed it up."

"How many are you?"

"Only four at the moment, but the house is open to everyone: there are always some girls coming and others leaving."

I coughed to clear my throat.

"And Marika, do you . . . do you know her?"

She paused briefly, then said:

"Sure I do."

"Is she all right?"

"She's just fine."

We were both on our knees beside Mr. Blue. The woman was wearing a blue turtleneck, patched jeans, and heavy gray socks. Her round face was smiling, and around her bright eyes there was a star-shaped sheaf of little lines.

I didn't have the nerve to ask why she'd hesitated when I mentioned Marika. I sensed in her, in her smile, but also in her whole attitude, a warmth that reassured me and put me at ease. I even felt glad she was there, because it was with a mixture of desire and fear that I'd been waiting for Marika to come, and the second emotion, I had to admit, had won out over the first.

I asked what she wanted to drink. She replied that she'd come to make a proposition.

"What kind of proposition?" I asked. "Honest or dishonest?"

"Dishonest," she laughed. "And as far as that drink is concerned, I think I'll change my mind. Do you have any rosé wine?"

"There's some Côtes de Provence . . ."

"That sounds fine."

While I was uncorking the bottle, she leaned on the kitchen counter and explained the proposition. She wanted to borrow a blowtorch and a cylinder of gas to do some soldering at the Girls' House; in exchange, she would come back with the girls, and they'd patch my leaky roof.

How did she know my roof needed fixing? I was about to ask when I remembered that I'd gone up on the roof the week before to assess the damage. Could it be that Marika, walking on the shore, had spotted me in the distance? . . .

While I was considering that rather unlikely possibility, an idea was taking shape in my mind: if the girls were coming to fix my roof, perhaps Marika would be part of the group . . .

I tasted the wine. It was delicate and just a little fruity.

"Madame," I said, offering Bungalow a glass, "your proposition isn't *too* dishonest. In fact, I'd even say I have a lot to gain from it."

"We'll see about that." She smiled.

Her expression was mysterious, but I didn't pay much attention to it. I liked more and more the little stars that appeared around her eyes when she smiled.

I showed her around downstairs, the bedroom upstairs, even the attic where I worked. And then I took the glasses and the wine and led her to the sun porch, where she told me how she'd got the name Bungalow.

For twenty years she had lived in the suburbs with her husband and her three children. Their bungalow was equipped with every convenience imaginable, from dishwasher to computer; the basement was finished, the property was landscaped with trees, flowers, a honeysuckle hedge, a swimming pool, and a small vegetable garden. Her husband was a senior civil servant with a big salary, and the children were attractive and bright. They had a dog named Whisky. In short, she had everything she needed to be happy, yet she wasn't; she felt that she was living in a gilded cage. Her life struck her as so monotonous that on her nineteenth wedding anniversary, she told her husband and children that she was leaving the following year on the same date. No one took her seriously, but a year later, after twenty years of "good and faithful service," she left home and went to live by herself in Old Quebec. And a few weeks later, she had established the group of girls.

When she talked with the girls, she sometimes thought about her house and her children, and on occasion she would sigh: "When I was living in my bungalow . . ." And that was why the girls nicknamed her Bungalow.

On the sun porch, we drank our wine while she went on talking about her past. I sensed something wistful in her voice, but she had a sense of humor that offset the sadness in large measure, and the rest was washed away in the rain that now was coming down on the river in a deluge.

THE GOOD-NATURED
OLD MAN

I waited all week for Marika to come and visit, but in vain. Ten times a day I leaned out the attic window, hoping to see the woman I'd invited, the woman who was creating such a strange turmoil in me, on whom I was counting to bring my story back to life.

At times, I thought I had spotted her in the distance, but it was only a shadow among the rocks, or a dog that had wandered onto the sandbar, or else it was all in my head.

While I was waiting, of course, I couldn't write. But I went up to the attic every morning anyway and stayed there till midafternoon; I remained at my post. And I was not unhappy. Solitude didn't really cause me pain. Actually, though I seemed to be alone, I wasn't really:

while I paced, I carried on lengthy conversations with friends who were scattered in places as varied as Key West, San Francisco, the Îles de la Madeleine, the eleventh arrondissement in Paris, the suburbs of Prague, a hillside in the Rhône valley, a village near Heidelberg in Germany; I would ask them questions and they would tell me about their growing children, their plans for next year, their sick parents, the weather, their lost cats.

And like everyone else I pondered the meaning of life, the existence of God, eternity, and all that. Unfortunately, the results of my reflections were very meager, and I couldn't even say if I believed in God or not.

During my youth, which had been saturated in a religious atmosphere, I had visualized God as having the features of a tired old man with a beard, who had no sense of justice and who was ready to forgive all human frailties because of everything he had seen . . . But did He really exist, that good-natured old man? And if so, did He have anything to do with me in particular? And what about me, did I have any particular relationship with Him? Did I talk to Him? And what about Marika? Did she, in the secrecy of her cave, when night came and her lamp cast shadows on the wall, did she sometimes talk to someone?

When you get right down to it, the only thing I'd always believed in was the soul. I was certain that I had a soul. We all did, even old Mr. Blue. While I was pacing the attic, I'd begun to elaborate the theory of the soul.

According to my theory, the soul was located not inside the body as was generally believed, but outside. It was bigger than the body and enveloped it and kept it warm. It had a slight bluish cast that could sometimes be seen in the dark. It resembled a long nightshirt, light, transparent, and diaphanous. At the moment of death it departed the body and drifted in the air for a while, like a ghost, before it went to join the other souls in heaven.

LA PETITE

When the girls arrived the following weekend to repair my roof, I was disappointed once again: Marika wasn't with them. Along with Bungalow, who brought back the cylinder of gas, were a very gentle, chubby, dark-skinned girl named Minou, a tall thin one whose name I didn't catch, and a funny girl, very young and skinny, whose face was half hidden by a mop of blonde hair, who I thought at first was a boy and whom the others called La Petite.

In midweek I'd gone into town and bought tar, asphalt shingles, and tarpaper. The girls took these supplies and some tools, and I led the way onto the roof, going through an attic window. I showed them where the water came in during heavy rainfalls. They told me then that they could manage just fine on their own and refused my offer to help, only asking me to prepare a good meal, which they'd enjoy once the job was done.

Before going down to the kitchen, I looked out at the river and saw at once that the sailboat was gone. Bungalow told me not to worry: Marika had probably gone out on the river to see if her hull was watertight; it was possible that she'd come back fairly soon to give them a hand. On that occasion and later while we were eating, I noticed that whenever I asked a question about Marika, the girls looked at Bungalow and let her answer.

The Girls' House, in Old Quebec, became a public establishment – an official shelter for women in distress – and Bungalow, who was its manager, wasn't able to visit me often. On the other hand, I saw more and more of La Petite.

She always turned up unexpectedly. She reminded me of the stray cats that came in through the basement window and shared Mr. Blue's food. As she usually rode her bicycle, I didn't hear her arrive; I would suddenly find her on the beach, in the kitchen, or in an upstairs bedroom. The place she liked best was my young brother's room, which still contained some toys and children's furniture. One morning, on my way up to the attic to work, I heard a sigh or a moan coming from the bedroom, and I gently pushed open the door. With her knees to her chin and her thumb in her mouth, La Petite was curled up fast asleep in the child's bed, the little bed with iron bars that looked like a cage.

She came to see the animals, not me. She had a special relationship with them. Not only did she know birds and was able to identify them by their songs, but squirrels and chipmunks would come and eat from her hand. When she went walking on the beach, all the cats would follow her, even big Samurai. She wanted to tame a groundhog that lived in a hole at the foot of the cliff; she boasted that she had tamed a porcupine. That may have been an exaggeration. La Petite didn't always tell the truth. When she came back from her walks on the beach, for instance, she would often talk about Marika, telling me she'd met her at the cave or on the sandbar and that she'd talked to her, when I hadn't even seen her yet. It's not that she lied, but she sometimes took refuge in an imaginary world. She needed to transform reality a little.

But there was one thing I liked a lot: she enjoyed surprising me. For example, she would disguise herself. She would put on old clothes that she'd found in a closet, then she'd walk through the house or on the beach, laughing like a loony at the stunned look that flashed across my face when I had the illusion I was looking at my brother or my sister.

OLD COLLIE

These visits from La Petite were to change a number of things in my life. The first of these changes was a happy one: the love story I was writing in the attic, which had got bogged down, took off again.

In the little bar in Old Quebec my characters, who had been frozen as if in a wax museum, started moving again. The woman sitting at the bar turned around, my hero finally saw her face, and except for a few details, it was . . . the face of La Petite.

As I was describing the thin face that was both gentle and wild, with its hunted look beneath a lock of blonde hair, I couldn't help feeling guilty. I felt dishonest, as if I were cheating. And yet I was old enough to know that since art is, by definition, artificial, the writer builds his work from whatever components he comes upon, and that the only rule that binds him is that of plausibility.

Basically, I was delighted that my story was moving again. Everything was going well. The woman finished her drink, left the bar, and walked down rue Sainte-Angèle. She was going toward rue Saint-Jean, with my hero following close behind. At the corner of the street, she hesitated and paused for a moment. She looked around and when the man had caught up with her, she asked him something. I was surprised to note that she had a foreign accent: very soft and musical, Czech perhaps, or Polish. The man answered her question and they strolled away together. Farther down the street, they turned onto rue de la Fabrique. They were on their way to the Terrace, the Château, the river, and I was with them all the way. The sun was just warm enough, it was perfect. Marlene Dietrich's song was still in my mind.

It was a beautiful day of writing and sunshine, and when I came down from the attic late that afternoon, I was tired, famished, and happy. Nothing bad could happen to me, I was invincible, and I had all the patience in the world for answering La Petite's questions. She'd come looking for me in the sun porch, where I was sipping a glass of wine. She'd taken the old photograph album from the walnut writing desk and she had a long list of questions.

"What's that?" she asked.

"That's the house when it was still a cottage."

"Was it in the village?"

"Yes."

"That man, is he your father?"

"Yes, he is."

"What about him, is he your brother?"

"No, that's a little neighbor."

"Who's she?"

La Petite was curious about everything. She turned the pages of the old album unbelievably slowly; we were advancing at the rate of two or three pages an hour, because she would put her finger on every picture and ask all kinds of questions. We were comfortably ensconced in the wicker love seat with the floral cushions at our backs, our feet on the window ledge. Her legs were stretched out, mine slightly folded: that was a minor difference. There were more important ones, such as the fact that she was sixteen or seventeen years old and I was over forty, but when my work had gone well, I was capable of forgetting certain painful aspects of reality.

She turned the page and put her finger on the picture of old Collie.

"Who's that?" she asked.

"Our dog. His name was Collie."

She said the name aloud to see how it sounded when she called: "Col-lie! . . . Col-lie! . . . Col-lie!" Her voice was so sweet and gentle that it turned my heart inside out, and old Collie's soul, which was drifting in the great celestial kennel of the S.P.C.A. for all eternity, could not have been insensitive to her call.

"What was he like?"

"Old and gentle. He was black with a white spot on his chest."

"How old was he when . . . ?"

"Sixteen," I said. "He was nearly blind. He'd fallen in a hole so my father came to see and then he went and got his . . ."

La Petite was watching me closely. I coughed a couple of times, trying not to succumb to the queasiness that was coming over me.

"You're sure he was too old and couldn't live any longer?" she asked suspiciously.

"I don't remember very well," I said. "I was just a child."

"I remember every single thing that happened when I was little . . ."
She put her finger on another picture.

"Who's that, your brother?"

"Yes, my little brother."

"The one you play tennis with?"

"Yes. His name is Francis."

"He looks like you . . ."

I took a closer look: she was right, he did look a little like me.

"And her, is that your mother?"

"Oh, no, that's the maid, Rose-Aimée."

"You had a maid?"

"Yes . . . but she was more like a second mother."

"She was? . . . Tell me about her, let's see."

Even though I was tired and hungry, I made an effort to plunge into my past, and my failing memory, which was running out of steam, brought some scraps of recollections to the surface. La Petite kept asking all kinds of questions, which I answered as best I could, because I could see what she was trying to do: having no real family of her own, she was doing all she could to construct one around us.

Fortunately, my work had gone well. The porch was flooded with sunlight, my soul was hugging me gently, and I had enough warmth to last me until night.

A SCALE MODEL
SUPERMAN

My relations with the river were ambiguous.

I was glad to know it was out there, just next door, while I was working. It provided, so it seemed, a certain strength and regularity for my poor inspiration. But with its boats, its tides, its gulls, its light, its changing colors, the river was much too distracting, so I made sure I could see only half of it: on the window ledge I'd set a bottle of water, a package of cookies, and a beer mug that held pens and pencils.

In spite of these precautions, there were still times when I looked out the window abstractedly instead of writing, and so it was that one day in mid-June I spied a female silhouette at the water's edge. It was moving toward the left. At first I thought it was La Petite, because she enjoyed strolling out there, but as I looked more closely, I saw that the silhouette was distinctly more slender. It must be Marika.

I tore down the stairs four at a time to get the binoculars from the kitchen. At any rate I thought I'd left them on the fridge, but they weren't there. Suddenly I remembered: they were in the attic, in the top drawer of my desk! . . . I raced back up the stairs, found the binoculars, and scanned the shore and the sandbar. The silhouette was still there, a little more to the left; then it moved away along the water's edge. It disappeared behind a rock, but I had enough time to see that it was barefoot and was wearing a long skirt with a white T-shirt.

Very excited, I galloped down the stairs again and went out on the beach. Then I came straight back inside to change into my cleanest jeans and a fresh sweatshirt. When I got back to the beach, I was out of breath, but I didn't even stop to rest.

Marika had disappeared from view. She must have gone farther away, to a place where the sandbar was bristling with rocks. I hadn't taken the binoculars, not wanting to seem to be spying. I began to run, but then I remembered that on the left side where she was heading, there was a very steep rocky cliff that blocked your way at high tide. And the tide was coming in quickly. Once she was at the end of the bay, Marika would be obliged to turn around. All I had to do was wait.

I took off my sandals, a souvenir of Key West, and left them on a rock. I went to the edge of the water in a leisurely way, avoiding the sharp rocks and stopping to dip my bare feet in the puddles of warm water. When I came close to where I'd spotted Marika from the attic window, I saw no footprints, but that was only to be expected because the tide had come in. I climbed onto a big rock so I could look toward the end of the bay. I couldn't see the silhouette I was looking for, but that wasn't surprising given the distance and the large number of rocks. I walked for a while toward where she had disappeared, then I decided to sit on the beach with my back against a rock and wait for her to come back. My legs were a little wobbly.

It wasn't long before I realized that my fatigue was partly due to the battle being waged inside me again, by my appallingly contradictory feelings: I couldn't wait to see Marika, but at the same time the prospect terrified me. Ashamed and annoyed at being split in two again, divided against myself, I resolved to ignore completely the feelings that were perturbing me. I tried to think about something else.

It wasn't my lucky day, because after that a familiar image came back, a painful one that often haunted me: it was the image of the bookcase whose shelves had gaps like an old brick wall because a young woman had taken away all her books. She had loaded them into boxes and then she'd gone away with a man who looked like Superman. He wasn't as tall or brawny, but his face really did remind you of that character. He was a kind of scale model Superman.

I wonder why images from the past, even when they're old and yellow and dusty, can cause us so much pain. Besides, that image of the bookcase was very persistent and I had to resort to an old trick to get rid of it. It's a trick that every writer knows: you simply make up your mind to include the image in a story you're writing. As soon as I'd decided to write that bookcase into my story, I felt a lot better.

Whatever calamities rain down on the writer's head, whether his wife is unfaithful or friends abandon him or colleagues envy him or creditors hunt him down, he can always take consolation from the thought that his misfortunes will become material for his next book.

I had come to that point in my reflections when the nearby lapping of the tide reminded me that time was passing and that Marika would soon be back. I got up to inspect the sandbar, which was becoming increasingly narrow, but I couldn't see anyone. I climbed up on a big rock again, and with my hand shielding my eyes from the sunlight that glinted off the river, I systematically studied first the rocks along the waterline and then the shore, which curved away in the distance like a shoulder, but there wasn't a living soul. I would have to wait some more.

I waited a good half hour. After that the tide had reached its highest point, and Marika still hadn't come back. I waited another fifteen minutes, and then who should turn up but old Mr. Blue. He was alone. He rubbed up against my feet and was obviously hungry. I decided to wait just five minutes more, and when he saw that I was staying, he started rummaging in a pile of garbage washed in by the tide: I realized from the smell that he'd found a dead fish or something of the kind.

The shore, which sloped slightly toward the water that now was touching it, was deserted all the way to the other end of the bay. There was nothing to do now but go back to the house. I stopped along the way to pick up the sandals I'd left on a rock. As I was inspecting the beach one final time, I saw old Mr. Blue go racing away.

FOUR MESSAGES

When I am writing a story, my soul becomes more opaque, I withdraw into myself, and I believe my life actually shrinks. Then I'm completely enslaved to my habits.

And so since the beginning of summer I had been getting up at half past eight every morning. I'd drink a glass of orange juice, eat some cornflakes with half a banana followed by two slices of toast and honey, and at nine I'd take a cup of coffee and go up to the attic. I would write until noon. Then, after lunch and a short nap, I'd go back to work and wouldn't stop until I'd written a full page. Until the page was finished, it seemed to me that I didn't have the right to live, I mean to walk along the beach to the sandy inlet, to drive around aimlessly in the Volkswagen, to eat a piece of chocolate cake with two scoops of ice cream, or to go and play tennis with my brother.

It would have taken something very special to make me miss a tennis match, even though tennis wasn't really a game for me. Rather, it was a set of rituals, a kind of ceremony, as I realized when I was inspecting my bag to see if I'd packed everything I needed: Reeboks, two pairs of socks, shorts and a T-shirt, two Yonex rackets, the extra grip, some yellow Dunlop balls, a box of Band-Aids, and supplies for a shower after the match.

To prepare myself mentally, I shut my eyes and thought about Martina Navratilova, the Czech player who was my idol at the time. I saw her rush to the net on the momentum of her serve and then, with knees flexed and body bent forward, she would drive a winning volley into a corner of the court. After that she would go back to the baseline, eyes lowered as if she'd just accomplished a very ordinary shot. However, an attentive spectator could see, very briefly, a satisfied smile flash across her face, to be replaced by a determined, almost fierce expression that revealed her somewhat masculine character. To see such determination and self-confidence, two qualities that were absent from my rather defensive play, helped me to improve my own game.

That afternoon, though, as I was getting my bag ready, my thoughts were not on Martina Navratilova: I was thinking about that slender silhouette I'd glimpsed for a moment on the beach. I wondered what would happen if Marika decided to come to the house while I was out . . . Was it not possible, in fact, that she might need some tool for repairing the sailboat? Or that she'd want to have a word with La Petite if, in fact, they were acquainted? Or might she simply feel like having a coffee or something? . . . You never know, so I wrote her a message and tacked it to the screen door.

Dear Marika,

I'm going to play tennis with my young brother Francis, but the door isn't locked. La Petite isn't here just now either; she must be out on the beach. Please come in and make yourself at home. I should be home by five.

Your neighbor, Jim

I went back to the kitchen for my tennis bag and the keys to the Volkswagen minibus. Before I took off, I decided to leave a second message on the table:

Dear Marika,

Thanks so much for accepting my invitation. Coffee and Nestlé's Quik are on the bottom shelf of the cupboard left of the sink; cookies too. Sugar and spoons are on the table in front of you. Milk and cream in the fridge. I'm very glad you're here.

Jim

After leaving this message conspicuously on the table, between the honey and the peanut butter, I picked up my bag and my keys, but as I was about to go out I couldn't resist the urge to write yet another note, which I left inside the fridge just in front of the milk:

Dear Marika,

If you prefer two percent milk, there's a liter on the bottom shelf. My cat didn't come in to eat at noon. Could you give him some Puss 'n Boots if you see him? The can is on the bottom shelf too. There's a very good apple pie on the middle shelf: please help yourself. You'll find vanilla ice cream in the freezer.

Jim

It was getting late. I grabbed my things and, after I'd climbed the path up to the minibus, I was running the engine, about to leave, when I suddenly realized I'd made a mistake. Marika would be arriving from the beach. As the minibus could be seen from far away when it was parked at the top of the cliff, she would see at once that it wasn't there. She wouldn't even come near the house, and she wouldn't see the first message! I took a quick look at my watch, then I turned off the ignition and galloped down the path again as fast as I could. At the house, I scribbled the following message:

Dear Marika,

The old Volks isn't there and neither am I, but come in anyway. It would gladden my heart to know that you'd come in and had a coffee or hot chocolate and some cookies, sitting in my place or standing and looking out the window. Just knowing you were there would make me happy. Even if I wasn't there myself. See you soon.

Your neighbor, Jim

Rushing out of the house like a whirlwind, I raced along the beach to a rock that was midway between my house and the scree. I positioned the paper on the rock and pinned it between two stones in such a way that it was easily visible to anyone coming from the cave. Without wasting a second, I retraced my steps and repeated the difficult climb up the cliff.

I wasn't late but I was tired when I arrived at the tennis club, my legs felt shaky, and I lost the match to my brother. On the way home I felt old, as if I were falling into ruin like the house. The four messages were still in place, even the last, the one I had left on the shore. I thought at least that one could have disappeared, blown away by the wind or picked up by a gull or who knows what.

THE SNARES OF LOVE
AND TENDERNESS

One night, La Petite sat on the floor of my young brother's bedroom and told me about her childhood.

"I thought he was allowed," she said, finishing her story.

"Why?" I asked.

"He was my father," she said. "I mean . . ."

Her small, slightly hoarse voice broke.

She was sitting in a corner with her arms crossed, and old Mr. Blue was lying in her lap. I sat opposite her, my back resting against the child's bed. Her head was tilted toward her chest so that her eyes were completely invisible. Usually, you could see one eye at least, the other being hidden by a lock of hair, but that evening when she talked about her devastated childhood, her tousled hair covered most of her face.

She made me think of a cornered animal.

"He was my adoptive father," she said. "I came from the Children's Aid. My real parents left me there when I was a little girl. I was five years old."

"Do you have any brothers or sisters?"

"No. I was all alone."

"What about your mother, I mean your adoptive mother, did she say anything?"

"No."

"Was she afraid of him?"

"I don't think so," she said. "Not afraid, but she thought he needed too much . . . too much affection, so she didn't mind me taking her place. Bungalow explained it to me. Do you understand?"

"Of course."

"I wasn't afraid of him either," she went on, petting old Mr. Blue.

"You weren't?" I asked, somewhat surprised.

"It's hard to explain," she said, "but I'll try. He was always nice to me. He didn't beat me or threaten me or anything like that. He had a soft, deep voice and he told me we were living a love story, a story like Tristan and Isolde, and that no one in the world would understand us. I was a prisoner of all that tenderness around me. I couldn't rebel, I couldn't do anything. It was like being caught in a trap. I was only twelve years old. Can you understand?"

"Yes, I can," I murmured.

She lifted her head briefly to look at me and picking up the cat in both hands, very delicately, like a woman lifting a baby, held it against her chest. I was ill at ease. All I could do was listen to her, my heart turned inside out, hoping she wouldn't start to cry, because I had no idea how to console her – I, a man, and probably the same age as her adoptive father . . .

I knew that I could trust Mr. Blue. He was behaving very well. He seemed to know exactly what to do: he was curled up against her and purring, showing her how much he liked being petted by her. He was telling her in his own way that being gentle isn't necessarily a disaster and that she mustn't despair of humanity.

Finally, La Petite became calmer and I went down to the kitchen to make hot chocolate. I was afraid Mr. Blue would be tempted to follow me, but he quietly stayed behind. When I came back carrying the two mugs in one hand and a bowl of milk for the cat in the other, she asked me to sing to her. I set the mugs and the bowl on the floor, made an effort to concentrate, then I started singing "L'Eau vive" by Guy Béart. She looked up again and I could see that she was smiling because her name occurred in the song: "Ma petite est comme l'eau, comme l'eau vive." It was an old song that I used to be very fond of, and I was careful not to sing off-key. Old Mr. Blue lapped up his milk while I sang. When I'd finished, La Petite sipped some chocolate, then said:

"Now you tell me something."

"You mean something about my past?" I asked.

"That's right, the first thing you can remember . . . Why are you laughing?"

"I'm laughing because when I was a professor, one of the essay topics I used to give my students was 'Your Oldest Memory.'"

"I know that," she said.

"How?"

"I was looking in the chest . . ."

"The one in my bedroom? The old leather chest with gilt hinges?"

"Yes. Are you mad at me?"

I paused for a long sip of chocolate.

"No," I told her. "I'm not mad. It doesn't matter."

"I should have asked permission?"

"Ye . . . Yes!" I said hesitantly.

Old Mr. Blue, who had drunk up all his milk, rubbed his whiskers with the back of his paw, then he stretched and went to lie in her lap again.

"May I have permission to look through the old chest?" she asked in a barely audible voice.

"Of course," I said.

"Thanks very much. Now tell me your oldest memory, please."

My memory is very peculiar: I forget most things, but I retain some strange details. My most distant memory goes back to when the frame house, though it was already old, hadn't yet made its famous journey down the river on the flat-bottomed boat that transported it here, to the middle of the bay, where, ever since, it has been resting its battered carcass against the cliff.

The house was still in the village then, on the bank of a small river, and it was a time of games that had no end and no frontiers, games that were not an essential part of our life, but life itself. One day, right in the middle of a tough battle between cops and robbers, I lost my footing when I was tearing down a steep, rocky path that ran through a vacant lot behind the house. I landed headfirst and hit my left knee on a pointed rock, and I ended up with a deep gash above my kneecap. My leg was covered with blood when my father, who had been told immediately what happened, picked me up to carry me home.

What I remember most clearly is that my father was wearing a white shirt that the blood pouring from my cut stained with red. What tormented me was neither pain nor apprehension about dying, but an irrational fear that he would be angry with me.

That adventure left me with a small scar above my knee (you can see it now if you look very closely), and the impression, if not the certainty, that my fear was excessive. Though I searched my memories, nothing about my father's usual behavior seemed to justify such a strong reaction. If he sometimes grew impatient, even flying into a rage that made everyone around him tremble, I also remember seeing him laugh at times when he could have lost his temper. Why, then, had I been so terrified at the sight of a red spot on his shirt?

"Maybe you were afraid he wouldn't love you anymore," said La Petite.

"Do you think so?"

"Yes, I do. You needed affection."

She drained her hot chocolate and went on:

"When we're little, we always need affection. Don't you remember?"

"Yes, I do, I remember. Why did you say that?"

"Because . . . because you're older," she said, searching for her words.

"I see!" I replied, rather offended.

She took the cat in her arms and, to make up for what she'd said, asked:

"Don't you think of yourself as old?"

"I'm old on the outside and young inside."

She thought that over for a moment.

"Maybe it's . . . maybe it was the same for my adoptive father?"

"I have no idea about that, but there's no excuse for what he did."

"You're right," she said. "I hate him now. I could kill him. I hate all adults except you and Bungalow . . . and a few others."

She launched into a long tirade against adults, and I felt shivers down my spine when she described the fate she intended to inflict if she ever got her hands on some of them. I knew that such belligerence could be healthy, and that it was most important for her to express her feelings. This was no time to tell her that, even for older people, the need for affection was still immense, infinite, out of all proportion to reality, and eternally unsatisfied.

I listened to her, saying nothing, as I sipped the last, rather bitter mouthfuls of hot chocolate. Just as I was starting to worry, her anger dropped abruptly. She heaved a long sigh and was silent, and then we heard nothing but the purring of old Mr. Blue, who had fallen asleep in her arms.

THE SCENT OF A
FIELD OF CLOVER

The first thing I did when I went up to the attic at nine every morning was to reread the page I had written the day before. As I'd deliberately stopped in the middle of a sentence that was already fully constructed in my head (a trick I'd picked up from old Hemingway), rereading it gave me the momentum I needed to start the next page right away.

Some days, there was a surprise in store for me: when I reread what I'd written the day before, I discovered that the sentence I'd left dangling had been completed and that several more had been added. Someone had gone up to the attic during the night and written a part of my story in my place . . .

Needless to say, that's not true. I'm joking! Nobody came and wrote my book while I was sleeping, but a phenomenon did occur that, while fairly common, was strange nonetheless; there were even times when I had the impression that someone other than I was the author.

In July, that loss of control was so pronounced that the situation became intolerable. Relations between my two characters (the man and woman who'd met in a bar in Old Quebec) started to take a direction that I didn't like at all. After their first meeting, they had seen each other several times in Old Quebec, where the summer festival was in full swing, and they'd walked through the streets, looking at the clowns and musicians, sat on café terraces talking about books and films and their travels; they drew out as long as possible the delicious pleasure we always experience when we meet a person we like and with whom we discover that we have a lot in common.

And now suddenly instead of becoming deeper, the ties between them had turned to friendship. It was a very tender friendship, one that had its own appeal and was fairly easy to describe, especially because I could use some of my conversations with La Petite. In the end, though, it took me away from my goal, which was to tell a love story.

When you start to write a story, you're like a traveler who has spied a castle in the distance. In the hope of arriving at it, you take a little road that descends a hillside toward a forest-covered valley. The road narrows and becomes a path that is obliterated here and there, and you're no longer very sure what place you've come to; you feel as if you're going in circles. Now and then, you walk through a clearing flooded with sunlight, or you swim across a river. When you emerge from the forest, you climb a small mountain. At the summit, you catch sight of the castle, but it is on the next hill and it's not as beautiful as you'd thought: it's more like a country house or a large villa. You don't lose heart, you descend once more into a valley, you take a nearly invisible path through a dark forest, then you climb to the top of the hill and, on your last legs now, you finally arrive at the castle. In reality, it's not a castle or a villa or even a country home: it's just a dilapidated old house that, oddly enough, looks very much like the one in which you spent your childhood.

Not wanting to get onto the wrong track, for a few days I broke off my work in the attic, where it was becoming unbearably hot in any case, and spent most of my time walking along the water. Old Mr. Blue came with me when the lovely Vitamin or his friends the stray cats weren't around, and sometimes it was La Petite who accompanied me, with her unsociable air and her questions about the past.

When I was by myself, I'd go walking with a book under my arm, to mask the awkwardness I expected to feel if I ran into Marika. For needless to say, it was she I was thinking of when I went out onto the beach. She still hadn't answered my invitation and I wasn't sure what my next move should be. I hadn't gone back to the cave; I had only verified from a distance to see that she hadn't finished repairing the sailboat. Secretly, I hoped to run into her by chance when I was on one of my solitary walks.

But the days passed and the chance encounter hadn't occurred, so

I had no choice but to go to the cave. On the day I decided to visit her, the forecast was for very hot weather, so I left the house immediately after breakfast. Mr. Blue was away (I hadn't seen him for two days), and La Petite, who had slept in my brother's bedroom, wasn't up yet. I quietly closed the door of the house.

As a child, I often used to play in the cave with my two brothers and my sister; of course we called it "Ali Baba's cave." In the little room at the back, safe from the high tides, we left fishing rods, dry wood, old inner tubes, diving masks and fins – and all sorts of things: it was our private place, our dominion, our territory.

Recalling that time as I headed for the cave helped make me feel less like an intruder. And on the morning in question, my soul was light and limpid, almost ethereal, and I was walking at a brisk pace. There was no question of letting my usual doubts sweep over me, because this visit was different from the others. This time, instead of going to see Marika out of curiosity or to ask her something, I had a little present for her: something written by Paul Hazard. When I was doing research on *The Arabian Nights* at the Laval University Library, I'd fallen in love with this text and made a photocopy of it. Later, back at the house, I had carefully transcribed it onto stationery and slipped it into an envelope.

I didn't even stop at the scree to assess the situation and mull over what I was going to do. The sailboat was in the cove, tugging at its anchor slightly because the tide was going out, and there was no sign of activity onboard. I headed straight for the cave: at this hour of the morning there was no doubt that Marika was there, as was indicated by the rowboat that sat on the beach, partly out of the water. Just before going inside, I took a deep breath and called out very loud: "Hello! . . . Excuse me!" then I immediately slipped in through the breach, holding my envelope in my hand.

The first room was empty, but I immediately recognized a very particular odor . . . one that I'd smelled before in country fields. My voice was unsteady as I asked if anyone was there. No reply. I picked up the oil lamp and went into the small room that served as a bedroom. No one. Marika wasn't there. It was hard to believe.

And yet there was that very special scent . . . It was everywhere and it took me a few moments to understand where it was coming from: the sleeping bag. Instead of being rolled up as it had been the last time, it was now wide open. It seemed to be still warm from someone's presence. I brought the lamp closer for a better look. The bag, which was khaki colored, had been used a lot, that was obvious from the spruce-gum stains, some charcoal smudges, and some seams that were mended with heavy black thread. It was what is called a "mummy bag," that is, it was shaped like a person: you could see the outline of the head and the rounded shoulders, then the bag narrowed toward the feet.

I hesitated briefly, then I bent down to sniff the odor that came from it. I searched in my memories . . . and all at once it came back to me: it was the perfume you smell when you're lying in a field of clover on a fine summer day.

I went back to the big room with the lamp. On the rocky ledge the copy of *The Arabian Nights* lay open, and I was surprised to see that Marika was one-third of her way through the book. She was at the "Tale of the Loves of Camaralzaman, Prince of the Islands of the Children of Khaledan, and Badoura, the Princess of China." I knew this story well: Prince Camaralzaman was in love with an "unknown lady" whom he had found at his side when he wakened one night, who bore a strange resemblance to him. She had disappeared and now he was searching for her far and wide, but everyone told the prince he was dreaming.

Before I left the cave, I took the passage by Paul Hazard from the envelope and put it beside the book. I took time to reread it, because I liked it very much. A little long, perhaps, but I really did like it a lot; I liked his choice of words and I liked his punctuation:

When Scheherazade undertook to tell her nocturnal tales and tire-lessly began to unfurl the infinite resources of her imagination, stoked by all the dreams of Arabia, of Syria, of the vast Levant; when she depicted the Orientals' habits and customs, their religious ceremonies, their domestic practices, everything about their vivid variegated life; when she pointed out how one could hold on to men and fascinate them, not through learned deductions or through the powers of reason, but through dazzling colors and glamorous fables: then all of Europe was eager to hear her; then sultans, viziers, dervishes, Greek physicians, Moorish slaves replaced the wicked fairy Carabosse and the good fairy Aurora; then light and whimsical architecture, gushing fountains, ornamental ponds guarded by lions of solid gold, vast halls hung with silks or with fabrics from Mecca, replaced the palace where the Beast waited for Beauty to waken to love; then one fashion succeeded another: but what did not change was the human need for tale after tale, dream after dream, eternally.

SINBAD THE SAILOR

I went home feeling not discouraged but disappointed, and a little sad. My love story had stalled and I couldn't even get to see Marika. My failures were piling up.

It seemed to me that the house, which was leaning against the cliff as it always had, was trying now to cling to the old oak trees that surrounded it; it was more dilapidated than it had been at the beginning of the summer. Inside, I searched in vain for La Petite: she had gone away without leaving a word. Old Mr. Blue wasn't there either, nor was Vitamin, though she came often now that she was expecting kittens. I would have been happy to see a cat, any cat, even big Samurai.

I fixed myself a cheese omelet with toast and coffee, and I ate absentmindedly while I tried to find a solution to my writing problem. I tried all afternoon, while I walked or read or did housework – or nothing at all. It would have taken a brilliant idea, a stroke of genius, a sudden inspiration, or even something more modest: an inkling, an image, a memory – but I couldn't come up with a thing. I kept going back to the solution I already knew: a meeting with Marika. The longer that meeting was put off, the more important it became in my eyes.

By the end of the afternoon, my morale was so low that I even caught myself being jealous of Scheherazade; I envied her storyteller's talent and the wealth of her imagination. It was very obvious that I badly needed a change of air, so I called my brother to see if he wanted to play some tennis. An hour later we were on a clay court in Quebec City. After the match, while I was showering in the locker room, something occurred to me that, while it wasn't brilliant, still was interesting enough that I wonder why I hadn't come up with it sooner.

My brother already knew the general details of what had happened with Marika and the sailboat, and with the love story I was writing in the attic. Now, he owned a small sailboat himself (a sailing dinghy, to be precise), and I hadn't thought of it until now. So I suggested he take it out on the river and then, under some pretext or other – a breakdown, for instance – he would cast anchor near Marika's sailboat; he'd have a good chance of seeing her and speaking to her, and he could tell me all about it afterward.

He agreed without hesitation. There's no one in the world like my brother. You can ask him anything, he always says yes. He's both gentle and funny, and he doesn't look you in the eye because he's a little shy, but if you meet his gaze even briefly, you can see that his eyes are sparkling and that a kind of flame is burning inside him. I wasn't at all surprised when he agreed to my proposal. What did surprise me, though, was that when I told him about Marika, my voice quite unintentionally sounded bashful and self-conscious. Exactly as if I was in love with her.

We agreed that my brother would go out sailing on the river the next afternoon, and that we'd meet again the day after, at exactly six p.m., on the ferry that operated between Quebec City and Lévis. We had chosen the ferry in memory of long ago when we were both much younger and used to spend long hours and sometimes the whole night on that boat, talking about everything and nothing and reinventing the world.

Five minutes before the appointed time, my brother boarded the ferry. I'd been there for a while already, leaning on the railing of the upper deck, and he waved as he made his way along the pedestrian bridge.

As soon as he had joined me, I asked:

"Did you see her?"

"Sure," he said, without looking at me. "I'm famished . . . How about a hotdog?"

"If you want."

I followed him into the waiting room where the snack bar was, and he asked the waitress for two hotdogs. Now that I knew he'd seen Marika, I'd stopped worrying, I could wait. He didn't say anything. He was looking at some newspapers and magazines. When the waitress gave us the hotdogs and two Cokes in plastic cups, he took me out onto the deck to watch the starting operations. You could already hear the humming of the engine. A bell rang out, brief and clear, and then the gangways were lifted. My brother bit into his hotdog.

"Here's what happened," he said.

A sailor cast off the moorings and slowly the ferry left the wharf.

My brother said that with the wind from the west, he'd had no trouble getting to the sandy inlet; he had cast anchor a few meters from Marika's sailboat.

I knew he was telling the truth.

"I saw your boat," I said. "I was up in the attic with binoculars."

"To keep an eye on me?" he asked, with a look of false indignation.

"Of course not," I said. "I was concerned, and I wanted to see if you were there or not."

"And what did you see?"

"Hardly anything, it was too far away. All I saw was that there were two sailboats."

I finished my hotdog and sipped my Coke. The ferry started tracing a broad curve as it pulled away from Quebec City. My brother was looking toward the Terrace and the Château Frontenac.

"She wasn't on her sailboat," he said.

"Oh, no?" I replied.

"No, she was in the cave. She came out when I asked if anyone was there."

"Then what?" I asked, holding my breath.

"I told her I'd struck a log and that I'd stopped to see if my hull . . ."

"No! No! I mean: what's she like?"

"She's very beautiful," he said.

That observation made me very happy. I felt as if my soul was sighing with pleasure and that it was going to fly away.

"Is she fairly tall and thin?" I asked, thinking of the silhouette I'd caught a glimpse of by the water.

"She certainly is," he said.

"With slightly curly hair?"

"Yes. It's funny, but she looks a little like you and . . ."

He hesitated and I signaled him to go on.

". . . and at the same time," he said, "she reminds me of a singer from the old days named . . . what was her name?"

"Marlene Dietrich?"

"That's it."

"Is her face fairly bony, with hollow cheeks and prominent cheekbones?"

"Yes, that's her exactly."

We had reached the middle of the river and a refreshing little breeze was blowing. It was one of those moments when you feel as if everything is perfect and you wish that time would stand still. The ferry from Lévis was approaching, and when it was close by, a young passenger waved to us in greeting and my brother waved back. He was always very lucky with girls.

"What was she wearing?" I asked.

"Marika? A blue denim skirt and a white T-shirt. And she was barefoot."

"And what did you do? Come on, tell me!"

"I put on my mask and snorkel and went all around my boat, taking it easy, then I swam to the shore and told her the paint was scratched, but the hull wasn't damaged. Then she invited me to dry off and relax a little."

"And then?"

"I accepted. It wasn't cold in the cave, but it was a little damp. She made a fire and she lent me a big beach towel. And then we talked."

"What about?" I asked.

"The sailboat, the repairs . . . the river . . . traveling . . . And about *The Arabian Nights*."

"Did you notice how far back she was in the book?"

"Yes. She was at 'The Story of Sinbad the Sailor.'"

"Already! . . . Are you sure?"

"Sure I'm sure."

"What about my text? Did she mention it?"

"What text?"

"The text I left as a present! The wonderful text by Paul Hazard!"

"Oh, right! She said it was wonderful. She thought it was a marvelous present and she thanks you very much."

"She really said 'a marvelous present'?" I asked, unable to conceal my joy.

"She sure did," he said.

Again this time he wasn't looking at me. His eyes were on the Lévis wharf where the ferry was about to berth. A siren blasted, they made fast the mooring lines, and when the boat came to a standstill along the wharf, the gangways were lowered and the pedestrians disembarked at the same time as the cars.

We had to disembark also, that was the rule, and a sailor came up to remind us, but my brother knew him – he knew everybody – and the man gave us permission to make the return trip without setting foot on land.

My brother was still hungry.

"What kind of sundae do you want, butterscotch or chocolate?" he asked.

"Chocolate," I said.

He headed for the snack bar and I followed close behind. Just now I felt very acutely that the resemblance between Marika and me was extremely important, and that I'd make a mess of my life if I didn't take it into account. But that feeling only lasted a fraction of a second, like a flash in my mind, and then I experienced the same rather complacent pleasure I'd felt all afternoon because of the harmony between the sun and the water, and because of the warmth of my brother's presence.

THE OLD HOUSE,
JOURNEYS, AND THE SOUL

Over the next days, despite the intense heat, I tried very hard to pick up the thread of my story. In vain: I could no longer write. I love my work and I wouldn't change it for all the gold in the world, but when I can't write, I feel that I'm worthless.

I know now what I should have done. It was midsummer, vacation time for everyone, and I should have been glad to take some time off from my writing. I should have taken advantage of the break to do some repairs, paint the old house, take a trip, even do nothing but think about whatever came into my mind, such as, for example, the theory of souls that I'd barely sketched out.

It wouldn't have been a luxury to repair the house. While the roof no longer leaked, thanks to Bungalow and the girls, there were cracks in the wallpapered bedroom upstairs and in the wood-paneled walls of the kitchen: most likely the framework of the house was going weak. I hadn't come up with any better remedy than to prop up the walls with beams that were supported by the old oak trees that stood at the four corners of the house.

I don't think I would have taken on any major repairs in this heat. A trip, though, would have been nice. The sedentary life suited me only insofar as it facilitated my work. Between books, I had crisscrossed the highways of Canada and the United States at the wheel of the old Volkswagen minibus. I'd once had it shipped to Europe to travel to some countries there. Sometimes I even ended up writing on the road, and then the old Volks served as my house, restaurant, and office. Some passages that were set in Quebec City had been written on a beach in Key West, or on San Francisco Bay, or in a parking lot off the Autoroute du Soleil in France, or in a campground on a hillside of Florence, or in Venice near the airport, or in a suburb of Prague: I would draw the curtains in the Volks, put plugs in my ears, and write, safe from the outer world amid the bluish silence of my soul.

For the soul, as I said earlier, isn't inside but around us: it envelops us. It is pure white and transparent when we receive it at birth, but then it soon takes on a color that ranges from the blue of the horizon to ultramarine, depending on the temperament of the person to whom it is given. Though invisible, it can be glimpsed, like a kind of aura, at night or under very special circumstances. As it is drawn toward the sky, it tugs the body upward, forcing it to stand erect;

at night, it lets the body rest. Its main task is to protect the body, to contain its life and warmth; when it departs, the body becomes cold. Its destiny is to return to the sky, where it will regain its whiteness before it undertakes a new mission on earth. There are powerful ties between souls; in fact, there are such things as kindred spirits, sister souls that seek each other out and aren't content until they've found one another.

This theory was gratuitous: it was based on nothing, it owed nothing to anyone. And it was incomplete, coming to me piecemeal whenever I happened to think of it. To support my way of looking at things, I had done some research in the library at Laval University. I'd read a number of books, notably Plato and the German Romantics, but I hadn't learned very much. I had read some things that I liked very much, though, like this passage by Albert Béguin:

> It [the soul] is aware that it comes from far beyond its known origins and that a future is reserved for it in other spaces. When it encounters the world where it has come to dwell, it experiences the astonishment of a stranger who is transported among some far-off people. It is gripped by profound anxiety when it questions the extent of its domain: temporarily exiled in time, it recalls or senses that it does not altogether belong to this world, of exile. Bent over itself or turned outward toward the external world, it tries to perceive those secret melodies that, in the stellar spheres as well as in human depths, still speak in the accent of a longed-for homeland.

THE BLUE TILE SHOWER

What matters are the emotional ties that connect people and form a vast, invisible web without which the world would crumble. Everything else to which people devote the greater part of their time, looking very serious as they do so, is of only minor importance.

I was musing on that one morning while I was drinking coffee in the kitchen when the door opened softly and I was surprised to see Bungalow. She hadn't been here for a month.

"Good morning!" I said.

"Sorry I didn't knock first," she said. "I thought you'd be upstairs and I didn't want to disturb you. I just came to have a word with La Petite."

It was eleven o'clock, but I wasn't working: I still hadn't figured out how to continue my story. I was very glad to see Bungalow and got up to give her a hug.

"How are you?" I asked.

"All right," she said. "What about La Petite, is she here?"

"In the shower," I said, pointing to the bathroom on the main floor.

"How are you doing?"

"Not bad, but I'm stuck in my story."

"Has this been going on very long?"

"Three weeks . . ."

Actually, it was *two* weeks. And I'd said that in my plaintive tone, like a child who wants consolation. To make up for my lapse, I went on as if writing were a subject of no interest whatsoever.

"Tell me about the Girls' House," I asked briskly. "Everything working out the way you want?"

"Yes," she said, "but we have a lot to do."

"Is that why we don't see you anymore?"

"That's right."

"We thought you'd forgotten all about us . . ."

Bungalow wrapped both arms around my shoulders. She was taller than I was, and more solidly built, and it felt very good to be held close to her, to feel her muscles on my forearms and her heavy breasts against my chest.

"When you're a mother hen," she said, "it's for life."

"Once a mother hen . . ." I began.

". . . always a mother hen!" she concluded, laughing.

In the bathroom, the monotonous lapping of the shower stopped and La Petite's husky voice could be heard:

"I'd like the mother hen to come and dry my back."

86

A little too quickly for my liking, Bungalow loosened her arms and left me alone in the kitchen. To pass the time, or for who knows what other reason, I started to imagine she was still with me, that her arms were still hugging my shoulders, and that she was asking me exactly what was wrong with my story. She wanted me to tell her everything, from the beginning. Around her eyes, which were looking at me with so much warmth, were those stars that I liked so much, and I recounted the whole story in detail. And when I got to where it had got bogged down, a strange thing happened: just as I was explaining what was wrong, I suddenly got an idea that might get my story back on track. I jotted it on the side of the Kleenex box on the table. Now I would have to let it rest, wait till tomorrow to see if it stood up.

I mentally offered Bungalow my sincerest thanks. She was still in the bathroom, from where I could hear murmurs, whispers, scrubbing sounds, muffled laughter, little cries . . . And then La Petite's voice:

"Will the writer come in and see us?"

One reason why I liked to sleep in the little downstairs bedroom, which used to be the maid's room, was that there was a big bathroom right beside it. My father had put in a huge, luxurious shower lined in dark blue ceramic tiles, from a model he'd found in an old issue of *House and Garden*. The shower was so enormous that it didn't need a curtain, and you had to go down two steps to get into it.

When I walked into the bathroom, I noted that Bungalow had left her shoes in the middle of the room. She was in the shower with La Petite, and she'd wrapped her in a towel. It was a very big bath towel on which was printed a lion that looked about as fierce as a cat; in fact, it resembled Mr. Blue. In the towel, La Petite was almost invisible: all you could see was her unruly mop of hair and one eye that was visible over the top. Bungalow was leaning against the blue ceramic wall in one corner of the shower with her arms around La Petite, and she was briskly rubbing her back and the top of her buttocks.

La Petite raised her head slightly.

"Come here!" she said in a thin little voice.

I moved to the middle of the room.

"Closer," she said.

I came closer and she asked me to come into the shower, and I did, after I'd taken off my running shoes. It was hot in the bathroom.

"You have to watch very carefully," said La Petite.

"Of course," I said. "But why?"

"So you can see the proper way to rub my back," she said.

La Petite rested her head on Bungalow's bosom and, again, all I could see was her uncombed hair sticking out of the towel. I could hear her purring like a cat while the older woman held her and rubbed her back. But what pleased me most of all was that Bungalow, staring vaguely into space as if she were blind, was murmuring sweet words into her ear, in the universal language of mother hens.

THE MAILBOX

The next morning I woke with a start at seven o'clock, very wound up. Usually I sleep until eight at least, but that day I was impatient to see whether the idea I'd had the day before, for getting my story moving again, had really done the trick.

I put on my glasses and hurried to the kitchen to reread the brief sentence that I'd jotted on the Kleenex box. This was my lucky day: not only had it stood up, it was as good as it had been the day before! I could start writing again!

The idea was simple: since my characters were interested in friendship, not love, I would pretend to go along with them. I was going to introduce a second female character, who would be a friend of my heroine. Then there would be a meeting between this new character and my hero, and I'd see what happened next. This idea gave my characters several options: they could fall in love; they could become jealous and hate each other; all three could try to be happy together. For the time being, all I knew was that the new character would have Bungalow's features.

I gave Mr. Blue his breakfast and wolfed down my own. I was worried, I was rushing . . . Why was I rushing so fast? No reason, except my fear, after twenty years, that the words would one day stop flowing from my pen, and that I would find myself dried up like an old well; my fear was so acute that almost every morning I had a tightness in my chest and cramps in my stomach.

Carrying my cup of coffee, I went up to the attic, careful not to make any noise because, since I had gone to bed before Bungalow and La Petite, I didn't know if they were still in the house. Upstairs, I opened all the windows, turned on an old upright electric fan, and set to work.

I went downstairs only once, around ten o'clock, to munch an apple and some chocolate cookies and to make a second cup of coffee. On my way past my bedroom, I noticed without paying too much attention to it that someone had opened the gilt-hinged chest: it wasn't properly shut.

When I stopped working shortly before noon, I had written fifteen lines, or half a page. I was fairly pleased with myself, not on account of those few lines, since I sometimes wrote a whole page in the morning, but because for more than three hours I'd been so absorbed in my story that I hadn't let myself be distracted either by the movements of the river or by Marika's presence nearby.

It was to her, however, that my thoughts turned at once when I'd finished working. I was all alone in the house. Bungalow had left a note on the kitchen table to thank me for my hospitality and to say she was taking La Petite, who wanted to go into town to see her friends. Too tired to cook, I ate what was left of yesterday's ham salad, with some ice cream for dessert. When he heard me open the fridge door, old Mr. Blue came up from the cellar, where it was probably cooler, and I fed him a small can of sardines with a bowl of milk.

After a short nap, I went back to the attic, but not to work; it was too hot. I wanted instead to do something I'd thought about during my solitary lunch: put a mailbox on the beach. I wanted to use a dollhouse that had belonged to my little sister, and I'd have to make a few alterations.

I found the dollhouse in a dark corner piled with broken toys, old furniture, and assorted objects. It was a two-story wooden structure with a sloping roof, painted white and green. It still looked fairly presentable in spite of a coating of dust, and it was in good shape except for the shutters, whose hinges had come loose. My father had built it himself for my little sister, the summer when she broke her leg in a fall from a tree. My sister very generously allowed us to play with it too, and we had stood the little house in the sand and constructed a network of roads, bridges, and tunnels around it. Then we had added more houses, a service station, a church, a school, an entire village where, amid a concert of shouts and car horns, several families complete with dogs and cats, cars, an ambulance, and a huge fire engine with a big ladder all lived together.

I took the dollhouse down to the workshop in the cellar to dust it off and nail the shutters back in place. Then, because it looked more like a birdhouse than a mailbox, I decided to change it a little: I wrote LOCAL MAIL in indelible ink under one of the upstairs windows and then I cut a little flag from a sheet of tin, painted it white, and fastened it to one edge of the roof, leaving enough clay so it could be raised or lowered, as needed.

Old Mr. Blue accompanied me out to the beach. Along with the little house, I brought a sledgehammer, a hammer and nails, and a four-foot stake, at the end of which I had nailed a small horizontal shelf. I went to a rock that was about halfway between my house and the scree. Climbing onto this rock, I took the sledgehammer and pounded the stake into the gravelly soil until it seemed solid enough to resist the wind and tides. Then I nailed the little house to the shelf. The cat jumped onto the rock and studied the house with a puzzled look.

"It's a mailbox," I said.

He was obviously waiting for an explanation.

"I'll show you," I said, picking him up. "See, you drop the letter in here, through the window, and it falls inside. You lift up the white flag like this so the person the letter's addressed to knows there's some mail. The white flag is visible from a distance, so the person can just come here, open the door, and take out the letter. Understand?"

He mumbled something that could have been an affirmative reply, and I went back home without paying any more attention to him. I was reasonably happy with my day. Now I could get back to my story, plunge into it wholeheartedly, and ignore what was going on around me, and if Marika felt like communicating with me, she could always drop a note in the box and lift up the white flag.

PRINCE VALIANT

It was so hot that I went up to the attic wearing just my shorts and my Key West sandals. Every morning, despite the heat, I went inside my story, gradually enlarging the little world I'd invented. For the moment, things were going well.

My hero enjoyed being with the new female character very much. She was his age, unlike the other woman, who was younger, and he had quickly realized that they were in agreement about the essential things. He thought that she even resembled him physically and he felt vaguely, though he hadn't quite given it careful thought, that some old things were resurfacing in him, stirring slightly.

She had a big apartment on rue des Remparts, not far from the Louis-Jolliet Hotel, with a fine view over the Bassin Louise, the river, and the Île d'Orléans – one of the most beautiful landscapes in North

America. The apartment made you think of a garden or a greenhouse, there were so many flowers and plants in it; half a dozen cats lived there too. It was a quiet place, sunny and rather mysterious, and it held a great fascination for my hero.

And I, as usual, stuck close to them, behind the scenes of their imaginary world, observing them closely, my heart filled with hope. I wanted them to fall in love, of course, because my goal was still to write a love story. But I also hoped that they'd find new ways to communicate. Just what these "new ways" would be, I had no idea. I suspected they would not be in the area of sexuality: they would be different, novel, original, that was all I knew. I was searching along with my characters, because for me, writing has always been a form of exploration.

My hopes were mixed with fear, however, and I was working feverishly: every day, I kept expecting a note from Marika in the mailbox or an impromptu visit to distract me from my work and bring me back to reality. I was mistaken, though; the distraction didn't come from that side.

One night I was wakened by a familiar noise. I rose, grumbling, and after going to the bathroom, I went into the kitchen: by the glow of the Coca-Cola clock, which was as round and bright as the full moon, I saw that old Mr. Blue and Vitamin had knocked over the garbage can, and the floor was littered with the remains of the chicken I'd cooked the day before and with all sorts of other garbage. To my amazement, Mr. Blue wasn't eating: he was looking at the lovely Vitamin, and I had the impression he was watching over her because she was expecting kittens. I gathered up the sharp bones so she wouldn't hurt herself, then poured each of them a bowl of milk, which they lapped up noisily before disappearing into the cellar staircase. They seemed to be in a hurry. I swept up the kitchen, then fixed myself a hot chocolate and drank it while I stood and looked out the window absently at the river. Then I went back to bed.

Just as I was dozing off, I heard the sound of breathing in my bedroom. I couldn't see very well because the room was only feebly lit by the electric clock that served as a night-light in the kitchen, but I knew it was La Petite. For two weeks now, she'd often come into my room in the middle of the night: I would wake up suddenly and catch sight of her in the shadowy light, sitting on the floor in one corner, or curled up in a ball like a cat, on the rug beside my bed. She would stay there without saying anything, unaware, I suppose, that her labored breathing, almost a wheeze, was enough to keep me awake. Then at daybreak she would tiptoe out of the room.

La Petite was breathing very hard. Through my partly opened eyes, I saw that she was sitting in the corner near the old chest, and I had the impression that she was wearing one of my young brother's shirts. Her arms were wrapped tightly around her bent knees, and, as usual, her face was half hidden by her hair. Needless to say, I hadn't forgotten what had happened in her childhood with her adoptive father . . . What did she want? Was she testing her strength? Did she simply need affection? . . . I had no idea. Huddled in the corner with her hair covering her face, she made me think of a wild cat.

Suddenly she cleared her throat to get my attention, and I pretended I was just waking up.

"Oh, is that you?" I asked, sitting up.

"Yes," she said. "Sorry I woke you."

"Have you been here long?"

No answer. I switched on the bedside lamp.

"What's wrong?" I asked.

"I don't know."

"Aren't you feeling well?"

"I'm all right."

"Shall I make you a hot chocolate?"

"Yes, please . . ."

I was wearing just a T-shirt, a long one, fortunately, that came halfway down my thighs. And so I got up for the second time that night and prepared more hot chocolate. It was half past three by the big clock. When I brought the cups back to the bedroom, La Petite was sitting in my bed, her legs folded and the single sheet pulled up to her chin.

I was going to sit at the foot of the bed, but she lifted the sheet, inviting me to get in beside her. First I set the two cups on the bedside table, then I got in next to her, a pillow wedged behind my back.

"This is hot," I said, handing her a cup.

"Thanks," she said.

She took little sips, murmuring approval. I couldn't see her eyes at all now. Sometimes you can look in a person's eyes and know if the soul is pale blue, or dark.

"It's hot, but not too hot. It's just right," she said.

She drained her cup and handed it to me to set on the table, then she wiped her mouth with the back of her hand.

"That really helped," she said.

"I'm glad," I said.

I was drinking slowly. Sometimes I can sip a hot chocolate or a coffee for an hour. I thought La Petite was going to tell me what was wrong, and I was surprised to see her turn onto her side with her back to me, as if she were going to sleep. I heard her ask:

"Can I stay here with you for a while?"

"Of course," I said.

"The chocolate helped, but I still feel funny."

"How?"

"I feel as if . . . as if everybody's gone away and I'm a little dog they've left behind. Does that makes sense to you?"

"Yes," I said, thinking about old Collie.

"But that's going to change," she said. "Bungalow said she'd help me . . . We're going to try and find my real family. We'll do research in the . . . parish registers."

In a voice choked with emotion, La Petite recalled something from her early childhood. She was turned toward the wall so I couldn't hear her very clearly, but I understood that her real father sometimes used to take her to the shore of a little lake where he'd built a cottage. He would hoist her onto his shoulders and walk with her through the forest along paths that ended in a place where you could see the American border. One could conclude then, that she'd been born in a village near the border and that was why Bungalow wanted to conduct her research in all the villages near the border.

"I really like Bungalow a lot," she said.

"Me too," I said.

"She's *super* motherly . . . At the Girls' House, if I can't fall asleep, I get into bed with her, and we talk about all kinds of things. Sometimes she tells me what it was like to live in the bungalow with her husband and children and her dog, Whisky. I always feel good when I'm with her . . . But there's a funny thing that happens: my memories start getting mixed up with hers, and when I'm unhappy, it's hard to sort out what's mine and what's hers . . . Do you think my stories are boring?"

"Not at all," I said.

I sipped some chocolate. It was getting cold.

"I feel good with you too," she said, "but it's not the same. Bungalow is really like my mother. She puts her arms around me and tells me things that make me feel better. The other day when I was in the shower, she taught me a saying . . . a proverb or something like that . . ."

"A maxim?"

"Maybe that's it . . . Anyway, the saying was: 'A valiant heart can conquer all.'"

"That's a fine saying," I said.

"Do you really think so?"

"Yes, I do."

I didn't say that just to make her happy. It was brief, spare, compact, and you couldn't remove or shift a single word. It had all the virtues that Hemingway liked.

"There was a special reason why it warmed my heart," she said.

"What was that?" I asked, because she obviously expected me to.

"Because of *Prince Valiant*, a comic strip I used to read in my father's library when I was little. Did you ever read it?"

"Yes," I sighed.

I remembered it very well. The older we get, the easier it is to remember things and people we've known, and the places where we lived during our youth. The details we've forgotten, a threshold worn down by people footsteps, the pattern on wallpaper or a curtain, the color of an old velvet armchair – it all comes back to us more and more precisely, as if childhood was a country we're returning to after a long absence, and as if in reality the journey of life was merely a long closed curve at the end of which we came back to where we started.

"Are you asleep?" asked La Petite.

"No," I said, "but I shut my eyes because of some memories."

"I feel as if you're far away . . ."

She half turned toward me and looked at me briefly through the lock of hair that hung over her eyes. Then she rested her head on the pillow.

"Do you feel comfortable with me?" she asked.

"Yes, I do," I said.

That wasn't altogether true. She asked:

"Do you love me a little?"

"Of course," I said.

"Say it, please."

"I love you . . ."

That wasn't true, obviously, but I didn't want to disappoint her. I wanted to make her feel that life was a great source of warmth and affection, that everything was working out as it should, and that she had nothing to fear.

Reaching out her arm, she switched off the bedside lamp and I could tell that, with her back to me, she was moving closer.

"Slide your right arm under my neck," she said, raising her head.

I did as she asked. She dropped her head back on the pillow and I could feel the warmth of her neck on my arm. Then she asked me to put my left arm around her waist. She took my hand and guided it so that my forearm crossed her chest diagonally, then she put her hand in mine.

"Now," she said, "bend your knees and put them behind mine."

I bent my knees and arranged them in the hollows behind hers as she asked, and then I heard something like a purr.

"That's *super!*" she murmured. "Now I won't say another word. I'll close my eyes and try to get some sleep."

After a while, her breathing became more regular. I felt the warmth of her back against my stomach, and of her thighs on mine. Her skin gave off a scent that reminded me of Johnson's Baby Powder.

I didn't dare to move, because now she seemed to be asleep. Sometimes she shifted an arm or a leg, or else she shuddered. I was beginning to feel pins and needles in my right arm, which was wedged under her head, but I tried to keep still. It wasn't unpleasant to be with her, sharing her warmth, but my arm was falling asleep: I felt at once comfortable and uncomfortable, happy and unhappy – the way one always does in life.

When two people are together in a bed and holding each other close, their souls sometimes dissolve into one another, leaving their bodies free to communicate as much as they want. For reasons that are easy to understand, though, that couldn't happen now.

By dawn, my arm was numb and sore. And because of the two cups of hot chocolate I'd drunk, I have to admit that I needed to go to the toilet, badly. The more time passed, the more uncomfortable I became. La Petite was fast asleep. All night, I'd done my best to keep perfectly still. I valiantly resisted my urge to move until daylight entered the room and woke her up.

OLD RUNNING SHOES

If two souls are to be united, a certain number of special conditions or circumstances are required. Or else the two must be kindred souls.

When kindred souls find each other after a long separation, they become thinner, melting into one another, as I've explained, and from their union is born the greatest happiness that can exist on earth.

But earthly happiness, great and pure though it may be, is not made to last eternally: it may happen that after a few years, lovers will tire of each other, or become attracted to another person and one day decide to part. And when two people part after living under the protection and in the warmth of the same soul, a rift occurs from which you don't recover for quite a while. That was what happened when my wife went away with Superman.

She had packed her books into cardboard cartons. What made me sad was not just that the bookcase now looked like a breached wall, it was also because I lost the books of Gabrielle Roy, which were among my very favorite books in the world. I'd thought they were mine, but I was wrong: they all belonged to my wife, except for the oldest one, *Bonheur d'occasion*.

The cartons of books had been piled up by the front door next to some other cartons that were already there, and then my wife carried them one by one out to a small truck. Looking out the window, I had seen that Superman was there to give her a hand and that it was a rental truck from Hertz.

After closing the truck's sliding door, she had come and sat in the kitchen while I made coffee. It was a special coffee that I bought in Montreal on Saint Lawrence Boulevard, and it was so good that nobody believed it was decaffeinated.

I'd brought her a cup to her favorite spot, next to the window. All this was going on in a small one-story house perched on a cliff, and the window looked out on a broad expanse of land that went down to the river in a gentle, undulating slope.

I waited, not knowing if she was going to say something, if she was going to give any kind of explanation. But she was silent. Superman had stayed outside by the truck. I looked at her and told myself that deep down I didn't really know her very well, not as well as I could have after ten years together.

She was a beautiful woman, intelligent and determined, and I had no reason to criticize her for anything. Her face was strained, her expression obstinate as she looked out the window and sipped her coffee. A fine drizzle was falling, so fine it was invisible unless you looked at it against a dark background, such as the shed wall or the bark of trees. I felt no emotion, only a great emptiness.

In the end, she didn't say a word. That was probably the best way to avoid the why's and how's, the shouting, the tears, the confusion, and the loss of dignity. She got up and walked through the house one last time, saying goodbye to the two cats and their five kittens one by one and then to me, and after that she left. I heard the doors of the rental truck slam and its engine rumble.

It was at that moment that the rift occurred. I suddenly had a sharp sensation of cold. I was terribly afraid of being alone and I felt like an abandoned child. It was very hard to breathe.

I don't know exactly what came over me: I went and took refuge in our bedroom closet. I shut the door and there was just a narrow thread of light. And then, in the half-light, I fell apart: I cried without restraint for I don't know how long, gulping and shuddering. I remember that I felt like a castaway in the middle of a storm, and that there was a strong, familiar smell all around me: the smell of the old running shoes that sat on the closet floor.

TWO HEARTS

I didn't work on Saturdays: that day was set aside for activities that keep me in touch with real life. When I went up to the attic around ten o'clock that Saturday, it was only to look out the window. I wanted to see if the sailboat was still there and if anything special was happening on the beach. I'd been locked away inside my story for quite a while now, only coming out for short walks to the mailbox, where, as a matter of fact, I hadn't yet found any mail.

I didn't see anything special on the beach, and the sailboat was still in its place.

Before I went downstairs, I couldn't resist the urge to glance at my work. I finished the last sentence, which I had left incomplete as usual, and I wrote another without too much trouble, and the beginning of a third . . . and then I stopped. I was on the threshold of my story, on the doorstep, and I could still choose whether to go in or stay outside. Unable to decide, I put down my pen and went to the kitchen for a coffee.

While I waited for the water to boil, I heard a sound from my bedroom and I went up to the door. La Petite was there, sitting on the floor beside the old gilt-hinged chest, which was wide open. She was surrounded by all kinds of papers, among which I recognized my old lecture notes, and she was holding *The Old Man and the Sea* by Ernest Hemingway.

"I'm sorry," she said. "I couldn't help it."

"It's not serious," I said. "But I'm surprised to see you: I thought you and Bungalow had gone to do research in the parish registers . . ."

"She can't get away. She has to stay at the Girls' House today; a woman just arrived; her husband beat her and she needed affection really badly . . . So I came to see the animals."

"You did, did you?"

When she realized that I was a little annoyed, she told me that she'd spotted a family of raccoons at the top of the cliff: a father, a mother, and three little ones. They liked cookies and they were easy to tame. And then she asked:

"Did Vitamin have her kittens?"

"I don't think so," I said, "but I haven't seen her for a couple of days."

"I looked in all the bedrooms, then I came down here, and when I saw the chest, I just felt like rummaging around a little . . . Are you mad at me?"

"No, of course not," I said.

She held up the Hemingway novel.

"Is this a good book?"

"It's very good," I said.

"Then how come it's hidden in the chest?"

"It's not really *hidden*. I . . . put it aside, with some notes on Hemingway."

"Why?"

"Because of something that happened to me in the past. An old story."

"Tell me, let's see . . ." she said.

"It's really an old story and it's a little complicated," I said.

"That doesn't matter," she said. "I like all kinds of stories."

A painful return to my past wasn't exactly what I'd been hoping for at that hour of the morning, but there was no escaping: hugging her knees, La Petite was all set to listen to me, and her blue eye shining under the unruly mop of hair reminded me that the best thing to do was to speak frankly and tell the whole truth.

I asked her to come to the kitchen. While I was making myself a cup of instant coffee, I thought about my work waiting up in the attic with the sentence left dangling, and then I tried hard to concentrate on my memories.

"Back then," I said, "I was a professor. I gave lectures, and I was a Hemingway specialist."

"I know that, you already told me!" protested La Petite.

"You're right. I'm sorry . . ."

I was like a man who is sensitive to the cold and is hesitating about going into the cold water. I took a deep breath and decided to take the plunge.

"When my wife went off with Superman," I said, "I was absolutely lost and I didn't know what to do."

"Were you unhappy?" she asked, as she came and sat at the table.

"Of course I was," I said.

"Tell me what it felt like," she insisted.

Inwardly, I recoiled: her question struck me as harsh and cold. But I knew very well that La Petite simply wanted to compare my feelings with those she'd experienced herself, so I did my best to be precise.

"I felt all alone in the world. It was as if everybody had abandoned me and I was worthless. And besides, I was afraid of what the neighbors would say, but that didn't matter. The worst thing was feeling worthless. Does that make sense?"

"Yes," she said. "Thank you for explaining it to me. Now, tell me what you did."

"I was cold . . . chilled to the bone. The first thing I did was put on my old gray sweater."

"And then?"

"Well . . . I cried," I said.

"For a long time?"

"A day or two . . . Maybe three."

"That's not very long," she pointed out.

"You're right," I said. "It's not very long."

"And then what?"

"The pain eased up, so then I started thinking . . . I tried to figure out what was wrong in my life."

La Petite raised her head, and again I saw one blue eye shining. "And then?" she asked.

"I understood something," I said. "I understood that during my whole life I'd never really been in love. I'd only looked for affection. I'd done lots of things to make people like me, but I'd never loved anybody."

"Not even your wife?" she asked.

I hesitated. I'd have had to distinguish between love, friendship, tenderness, and all that, and I wasn't in the mood. I took a long sip of coffee and replied:

"There was always a lot of tenderness between us, and we were very comfortable together."

La Petite ran both hands through her tangled blonde hair, a sign that she was lost in thought. She repeated the word "tenderness" several times. She said it very softly, in a caressing voice, as if she were trying to tame the word. And suddenly her face lit up.

"Tenderness," she said warmly, "I like that a lot. Now tell me what you did."

"I made some major changes in my life. I left teaching and I started writing. And I traveled. I bought the Volkswagen and I began by traveling around the United States. Then I put the Volks on a freighter and went to Europe: I wanted to see the cities whose names I'd heard when I was young, in the old songs by Brel and Léo Ferré and – "

"Are you happier than you used to be?"

The question was a slap in the face as it broke into my rather conceited account, and I was disconcerted.

"I can't say," I said.

"Try," she said.

I tried in vain to collect my thoughts. I was neither happy nor unhappy. I was looking for happiness in an instinctive way, like everyone else, and it was getting away from me.

"I don't know what happiness really is," I said. "The best answer I can think of is in that book you had a while ago, the one by Hemingway."

"All right, I'll read it," she said. "But first I want you to explain something else. In your lecture notes you ask your students why one of Hemingway's stories is called 'Big Two-Hearted River.' You ask them to find 'the true reason' . . . Will you tell me the answer?"

"I'm sorry, but I honestly don't remember. I have a very bad memory."

"Try and remember . . ."

"It's been so long," I said. "I'd have to reread my notes."

"Do whatever you want," she said, "and take as long as you want."

Despite her youth, the girl was as stubborn as a mule; she never gave up. I started pacing the kitchen, stopping now and then to go to the bedroom and read some of the pages scattered across the floor. I wasn't really trying to think. I sensed that the words "two-hearted" stirred some slightly murky emotion in me, so it was better to wait. Sometimes the words come along by themselves: you just have to leave them alone, give them time. And then some images suddenly surfaced.

"I think it's coming," I said.

"That's good," she said, "but I'm not in a hurry. I can wait."

Among the images that offered themselves to me was a photograph of Hemingway: he was wearing a cap and a hunting jacket, and his belt was stuffed with cartridges. He had a double-barreled rifle under his arm, and he was posing proudly beside a buffalo he'd shot on safari. While I was describing the photo to La Petite, I explained that it was the best-known image of him, but that there was another, more secret one that I used to ask my students to find.

"That's hard!" she protested, ready to reproach me.

"Not all that hard," I said, "because I'd given them a reading assignment. If they read it carefully, they could find the explanation for 'two-hearted.'"

"Whereabouts?" she asked.

"I don't remember exactly, but there were three places at least. The first one was an interview with Hemingway's wife, Mary; she was asked what Hemingway thought about the legend that made him into a kind of superman, and her answer was that, for him, it was overdone and ridiculous and totally idiotic. The second quotation was from *Papa Hemingway* . . . but where exactly?"

Memory failed me. Luckily, La Petite remembered seeing the title in my lecture notes. She went to the bedroom, searched through the notes, and came back a minute later with a page.

"Here it is!" she said with a very satisfied look.

"You're right, that's it," I said.

It was an account of a brief conversation between Hemingway

and Hotchner. Hemingway was telling about the early days in Paris, when he was poor and his rejected manuscripts came back to him in the mail. He told Hotchner: "There were times when I'd sit at that old wooden table and read one of those cold rejection slips that had been attached to a story I had loved and worked on very hard and believed in, and I couldn't help crying." And Hotchner said, surprised: "I never think of you crying." And old Hemingway replied: "I cry, boy. When the hurt is bad enough, I cry."

That exchange didn't seem to surprise La Petite, who asked almost immediately:

"What about the third one?"

"That's the story about the owl," I said.

"Tell me, let's see . . ."

This time, no research was needed. I remembered this story very clearly and I was able to tell La Petite in detail. One day Hemingway had shot a snowy owl that was sitting high in a tree. The owl had fallen, but because it was only wounded in one wing, he established what he called a headquarters for it in his garage, fixing up a box for it that he lined and covered with old hunting clothes. Every morning at breakfast time, he brought the owl a mouse he'd caught during the night; he gave it water, worried over its health, and helped it learn to fly again. The owl had let itself be tamed and they'd become good friends.

"He's really weird!" said La Petite, scratching her head. "He likes animals, but he shoots at them. I don't get it. Do you?"

"I don't know," I said. "You find it strange?"

"Yes."

"Why? . . . Explain it to me."

This was of course an old teacher's trick: I wanted her to work out the answer herself.

"Has it got something to do with 'Big Two-Hearted River'?" she asked.

"That's right," I said.

She murmured: "Two-hearted . . . two hearts . . ." and went back to the bedroom to go through my notes again. When she returned, I swear I saw her face light up briefly again under the shock of hair, at the very moment when the truth came to her.

"I think I understand now," she said.

"Yes?"

"It was like old Hemingway was divided in two."

"Yes . . ."

"He was aggressive and he was gentle, so . . ."

" . . ."

". . . so *he* was the one who was two-hearted," she said finally. "Is that the 'true reason' your students were supposed to find?"

"Exactly," I said.

I was expecting to see on her face that look of triumph she always had when she was proud of herself, but now, on the contrary, she was frowning: she was still looking for something.

"Could you say that Hemingway had a masculine half and a feminine half?" she asked.

"I think you could," I said.

"And you think everybody's got a double heart like him?"

"Could be."

I looked at her face and this time I saw that she was happy. But she wasn't wearing a triumphant look, instead she had a smile of satisfaction that I thought was marked with great tenderness. She went back to the bedroom, probably to tidy up and close the gilt-hinged chest. As I was putting my empty cup in the kitchen sink, it occurred to me that I could go back up to the attic, but in the end I decided not to work that day, but to take advantage of the summer while the weather was settled and fair.

THE APPARITION

By August, the heat had not let up. One morning when I was still very sleepy, I was gazing absently out the kitchen window – when I realized that I could hardly see a thing! Not even the beach. I could barely distinguish the white blur of the four birches that huddled fearfully in front of the house. For a moment I thought the windowpane was covered with mist, but that wasn't the case: it was fog. The house and everything around it were wrapped in the thickest fog I'd ever seen.

It was a peculiar day. La Petite started dressing up again as she'd done at the beginning. Every time I came down from the attic for a coffee or something to eat, I would see her walking around in old clothes of my little brother's or my sister's. Lovely Vitamin, who had just had a litter of three tiger-striped kittens, confined herself to the cellar with old Mr. Blue, and the whole house seemed to have been taken over by stray cats that growled at each other, making sounds like a wailing child. And from the invisible river came the intermittent howl of boat sirens.

All that day I was unable to write. And yet I hadn't dried up like a well. On the contrary, I was troubled by all sorts of sensations and intuitions that filled me with an unfamiliar stirring, but it was all vague and hard to translate into words. I didn't really understand what was going on, but I felt different, a stranger to myself.

Around eight o'clock that night, I went outside to take my mind off things. It was still light outside, but the fog was so dense that I couldn't see ten meters ahead of me. I'd brought a flashlight, but the beam of light dazzled me when it was reflected off the mist as if it were a white wall, so I doused it. Old Mr. Blue was with me, and whenever we heard a boat siren, he growled.

I took a few steps along the beach in the direction of the river, then turned to the right. The old cat followed close behind as if he needed protection. I was going very slowly, looking before I set my foot down, and sometimes testing the ground with the tip of a branch I was using as a walking stick. For fear that the slope of the beach would take me to the water, which I couldn't see, I followed the almost uninterrupted line of wrack and debris left there by the morning tide. For once, Mr. Blue didn't explore the garbage: he clung anxiously to my legs, and I didn't feel very confident myself.

I had been walking toward the cave for ten or fifteen minutes when the cat, more and more agitated, started to growl and spit. This time it wasn't because of a boat siren. I pricked up my ears, stopping so

I could concentrate on listening better, but I couldn't hear a sound. A few moments later, though, I could make out some furtive slipping sounds and, from time to time, some cracks that sounded like footsteps.

Then suddenly the sounds were very close. Old Mr. Blue scurried off toward the house, and the only reason I didn't do the same was my fear of hurting myself if I should trip on a rock or a dead branch. Looking around, I spied on my left, several meters away, the mailbox and the rock on which I'd stood to put it in place. I quickly huddled against the rock and then, with my heart pounding, waited to see who was coming toward me in the fog.

There was silence for several seconds, when again I heard, very distinctly, the sound of footsteps. Then suddenly I saw the silhouette of a woman through the fog. She disappeared immediately, but this was no hallucination: for a moment I had seen very clearly a slender form dressed in a long white nightgown. I even thought I'd caught a glimpse of a thin, bony face, but for that detail I may have been influenced by the description of Marika that my brother had given me on the ferry.

I stood motionless, still huddled against the rock, long after the silhouette had vanished in the fog. The cooler air off the river made me shiver, and my mind cleared to some extent. Night had fallen. I switched on the flashlight and went home as fast as I could, pointing the beam of light on the ground ahead of me so I wouldn't be blinded by the glare. Back at the house I found old Mr. Blue lying next to Vitamin, who was nursing her kittens. The stray cats had all disappeared.

I went into each of the bedrooms and up to the attic, looking for La Petite, but she wasn't there.

Still shivering occasionally, from fatigue and from nerves, I poured myself a finger of gin and added some hot water and honey. Then I took my drink to the sun porch. The gin relaxed me, though it didn't calm the emotions I was feeling. Normally, the appearance of Marika, whom I'd been trying to see for three months, would have made me happy, or stirred contradictory feelings . . . This time, though, I distinctly felt fear, a very sharp fear that, in its physical manifestations, was close to anguish.

I don't know how things happen inside us, I mean in the very depths of our beings, but I'm certain that if someone had been able to look deep inside me on that foggy August night, he would have seen some peculiar beings: ghosts of the past, nightmare figures, giants and witches, beasts with sleepy eyes.

A NEW WORLD

I'm not very good at introspection. Generally what I do is glide along the surface of things like a drifting raft that knows nothing about what goes on in the depths of the sea.

And so I couldn't understand why the appearance of Marika had left me so nervous and agitated. Was it because the fog had made her look unreal, almost ghostly? Or because the apparition had awakened some disturbing or threatening memory? The second explanation seemed more plausible, because in the days that followed I remembered a number of events from the past. The one that haunted me most persistently had occurred shortly after my wife had left me.

When my wife ran away with Superman, I didn't stop thinking about her. I was obsessed by a desire to see her again, even after the pain of separation had subsided.

Then, one day I received a phone call: they were inviting me to spend the weekend with them in a cottage they'd rented at Les Éboulements. Everyone knows that if you want to take a summer break, there's no finer place than Les Éboulements and Saint-Joseph-de-la-Rive. I tossed some things in a bag and, without wasting a moment, got behind the wheel of the Volvo sports car I had at the time.

As I drove away from the little house perched on the cliff and into the countryside, as the sweetness of the air and the warmth of the sun poured over me, forming one with the sports car, I felt the bitterness that had stayed behind in the secrecy of my heart melt away. Driving was good for me: it consoled me.

Of all the roads I've driven, the one that's the most comforting, the most motherly, may well be the one that begins at Quebec City, goes along the north shore of the Saint Lawrence River, and takes you up hill and down dale through the Laurentians, the oldest mountains in the world, to Baie-Saint-Paul. A few kilometers past the town, still on the road that follows the water's edge, you climb a hill and then turn right at the sign for Saint-Joseph-de-la-Rive. Your astonished eyes are greeted by a steep descent that takes your breath away; you approach it cautiously, in first gear, with your foot on the brake and a tightness in your heart, at once anxious and marveling at the sight of a vast shifting landscape in which water, air, and land are mingled, where long barges seem to sail in the sky, where the islands in the river merge into the ships – a landscape in which everything makes you feel as if you're entering a New World.

To get to the cottage, I had to drive down that sheer hill, through

Saint-Joseph-de-la-Rive, and then, outside the village, along a dirt road that climbed up the side of the cliff. Superman and my wife were in the garden when I pulled up; they were sunbathing on a big air mattress, and they'd put on their swimsuits to greet me.

All afternoon we drank beer and wine, and talked about this and that, mostly literature. It was interesting and sometimes funny, because Superman, who was a painter, had read a lot of fiction and poetry and, since he was from Montreal, he'd hung around with the literary crowd and its tight circle of selective friendships and malicious gossip. My wife said little and smiled a lot, her expression timid, her eyes gentle, and she paid as much attention to me as to Superman. Late that afternoon, when the tide was almost out, the three of us walked down to the beach to the left of the wharf for a picnic and a walk along the sandbar.

At low tide the sandbar at Saint-Joseph-de-la-Rive is one of the longest and most agreeable ones I know. Before you is a vast expanse of sand, with pools of warm water that are kind to bare feet, and rocks you can sit on to rest and daydream as you look across to the Île-aux-Coudres. You are free to go where you want. You walk at random and after a while you are merely a small black dot on the sandbar, and you feel as if you've disappeared into the landscape. If you want, you can take off your clothes and walk in the sun as naked as Adam or Eve.

We walked for a long time, a very long time, in the sun that day, sometimes the three of us together, sometimes scattered, and when we got back to the shore, we were very hungry and thirsty. We wolfed down the food we'd brought, including a jar of olives and a huge bag of cookies, washing it all down with wine. A lot of wine. As a matter of fact, when we'd finished eating, we were absolutely drunk, and I myself, not a great drinker, was in such a state that I suggested to Superman and my wife that we go for a moonlight swim. Though God knows how I hate swimming in the cold water of the river.

They thought it was a good idea, but we had to wait for the tide to come in; and so, to pass the time, we drank some more wine and smoked some hash, and after that, I don't remember very clearly. I think I slept for an hour or two, wrapped in a blanket, and I don't know what they did during that time.

When I woke up, the tide was high. The full moon was so bright that the river seemed lit by a floodlight. Perhaps I was still drunk, but the water didn't seem too cold now, just a little cool. After our swim, though, I suddenly felt the cold seep into me. I began to shiver, my teeth chattering. I got dressed again, wrapped myself in a blanket, and even ran along the shore for a while, but I couldn't stop shivering. My soul couldn't warm me now. I was freezing to death. So then I shouted to the others that I was going back to the cottage, and I left.

Lying in bed in the guest room, buried under several blankets and a heavy quilt, I was still shivering, shaking like a leaf, when they came in. They exchanged a look, then quickly undressed and climbed into bed. They lay very close to me so that I could feel their warmth, but it wasn't enough. Then they stretched out on top of me, first one, then the other, Superman first and then my wife, and after a while I stopped shivering. I was starting to feel better. It was like a thaw: my muscles relaxed and I felt waves of heat sweep over my whole body.

After this thawing, all three of us were carried along by a great wave of desire and tenderness, the two feelings mixed up together, as were the hands and mouths and smells – a broad, powerful current like a spring breakup, one that carried not just pleasure but generosity and sometimes pain as well, and that finally abandoned us at dawn, on a strange shore, with our eyes smaller and our souls a little bruised.

CHICKEN AND HONEY

La Petite was fast asleep in my brother's little iron bed. I tapped her shoulder as gently as I could, but she woke with a start, pulling herself up on her elbows and looking at me like a hunted beast.

"Nothing wrong," I said to reassure her. "Everything's just fine. But it's time to get up."

She had asked me to wake her early that morning, because Bungalow was coming to pick her up and start their search through the parish registers. She rubbed her eyes with a little saliva (that was the extent of her morning toilet), then she came downstairs to the kitchen. Sitting across from me with her head down and her face hidden by her blonde hair, without a word she drank the orange juice I'd squeezed for her. She seemed not to notice that as a treat I'd stirred a little sugar into her glass. The only time she emerged from her silence was when old Mr. Blue jumped onto the table to drink up the milk from her cornflakes: she murmured to him some incomprehensible words that had the affectionate inflections of the language of cats.

Three blasts of a car horn – one long and two short – signaled Bungalow's arrival at the top of the cliff. La Petite flew out of the house, and I had to run after her to give her the paper bag I'd packed with peanut butter sandwiches, apples, and a thermos of coffee.

After I'd fed the cats, I took my cup of coffee up to the attic, where I tried to write. I hadn't been writing well for a week now. It's painful for me to admit, but I'd had the ludicrous idea of including in my story some love scenes involving three people, similar to the one I'd experienced with Superman and my wife. That idea, about which I can say in my defense that it had come to me during a barren period, had cooled the relations between my characters to some degree, and here I was once again moving away from the love story I wanted to write.

It was entirely my fault: short of inspiration, I'd introduced into my story the first thing that occurred to me . . . There are times when a writer can come up with nothing better than the wreckage of his own life.

That day and on the days that followed, in the hope of getting out of the impasse, I worked an hour longer than usual, but it was no use. The next morning, when I reread the few sentences I'd struggled over the day before, everything seemed flat and devoid of interest, so I crossed it out to make a fresh start.

As for La Petite, she came back to the house that night a little more disappointed than the day before. There was no need to ask any questions; her glum expression was enough to show that despite her efforts and Bungalow's, she'd found no trace of her real family. In a fit of pique, she locked herself in the cellar and spent hours there with Vitamin and her tiger-striped kittens. By the end of the week, it seemed to me that her face had taken on a yellowish tone like old parish registers.

On Friday night I decided to cook her some chicken with honey. I'm not very talented in the kitchen, and I'm not very interested in cooking – I could gladly eat spaghetti every day – but chicken with honey is one of two or three dishes I'm fairly successful with. It's easy: you just make a sauce from butter, honey, mustard, and curry powder, and baste the chicken with it three or four times while it's roasting.

La Petite came and sat at the table, dressed in a ragged old T-shirt and paint-spattered jeans. For a while now the kitchen had been filled with the aroma of chicken and honey, but she pretended not to notice. She dropped her paper bag on the table and took out a peanut butter sandwich she hadn't eaten for lunch.

"Don't you want some chicken?" I asked.

"I'm not very hungry," she said morosely.

"Not even a little piece?"

She shrugged, and I watched her peel off one slice of bread and spread an impressive layer of strawberry jam onto the peanut butter. Meanwhile, I served myself some chicken and mashed potatoes, covering it all with honey sauce. She squinted at my plate as I took my plate across from her, but she said nothing.

"I'm famished," I said. "I worked longer than usual."

"And what happened?" she said.

"Nothing: I didn't write a line . . . I tried all week to get my story back on track, but nothing's worked. I'm hopeless. The lowest of the low."

I was exaggerating. I just wanted her to say something, shake off her dejection. After a long silence, she looked up to see if I really meant what I was saying.

"It's not going very well for me either," she said. "We looked in parish registers all week and didn't find a thing. There are still two parishes . . ."

"Do you feel discouraged?"

"No. Bungalow said we've got a good chance of finding something. She says she has a premonition . . . Do you believe in things like that, in premonitions?"

"I know one thing I believe in: Bungalow is never wrong."

"That's true," she said. Her face, or at least the half of it that I could see, gradually brightened. "Good thing Bungalow's so sweet and patient with me," she said.

"Why?" I asked.

"You know, the birth certificates in those old registers are handwritten, so they're hard to read and I'm always grouchy. But Bungalow never gets mad, and she never seems impatient. I really think she's the sweetest person in the world."

She smiled briefly and I saw a gleam of satisfaction in her blue eyes. She asked:

"Can I make you an offer?"

"Go right ahead," I said.

"I'll trade you half my peanut butter sandwich for a piece of chicken with honey. Deal?"

"It's a deal."

She held out her plate and I served her some chicken with sauce and a small helping of potatoes, and she passed me half her sandwich in exchange. I bit into it, not without a certain apprehension because of all the strawberry jam, but it actually wasn't that bad, just a little too sweet. In any case I pretended it was a feast.

"This is very good," I said steadily, chewing thoroughly to avoid any digestive problems.

"Thanks," she said. She smiled again and something very gentle lit up her face. Her soul might have been sky blue. "The chicken's very good too," she said.

"Thank you," I said. "Would you like some wine?"

"Oh yes!"

"White or red?"

"White, please."

I took the bottle of Bordeaux from the fridge and set it on the table with two glasses, which La Petite filled. The wine was too sweet, more suitable as an apéritif or a dessert wine, but I rather liked it anyway: it was very helpful for getting me through that melancholy hour in the late afternoon when the daylight lingers before reluctantly giving up its place to the night, when all kinds of fears and memories assail us.

Offering me a glass, La Petite said abruptly:

"So your story isn't going very well?"

"I'm blocked," I said.

"What's wrong exactly?"

"I can't write any more. It's been a week now."

"I know, but . . . *why*?"

I didn't much feel like answering. It was Friday night, I wouldn't work the next day, and I felt more like resting my mind, thinking of nothing except maybe my tennis match with my brother. But La Petite was probably going to bombard me with questions until I told her the truth, so I explained what had happened in the past with Superman and my wife, and why I'd decided to put that experience into my story.

"So your characters did what you did with your wife and Superman?" she asked.

"Yes," I said. "Except that in my story there's one man and two women, not the reverse."

"And what happened?"

"What happened is that my characters become friends, not lovers. You see, I've been trying to write a love story and this is the second time my characters have ended up as friends."

"I can understand that very well," she said.

That girl surprises me sometimes. She seemed to think that what I'd experienced with Superman and my wife was quite normal, while with the intransigence of youth she could easily have been shocked. Besides that, she accepted with no argument the relatively little known fact that a novelist's character can get away from him.

She asked:

"What did you do the first time it happened?"

"I added a character," I said. "There was already a man and a young girl and I put in a woman . . ."

"And then what?"

"Then my hero was attracted to the woman. Everything was going fine and I was happy, and there was that triangle, just as he was about to fall in love with her, and the love was transformed into friendship."

"And you can't turn back, get rid of the triangle and pick up your story again where things were going well?"

"Oh, no," I said. "Writing is like life, you can't retrace your steps."

I was very surprised to hear myself say that, but the question was one I hadn't thought about at all. La Petite, however, was pursuing her ideas:

"And you can't add another character like you did the other time?" she asked.

"I don't think so," I said. "There are quite a few already."

"If that's the case, I don't really see what you can do. Unless . . ." She stood and helped herself to more chicken and potatoes and a lot of honey sauce. "Can I say something stupid?" she asked as she sat down again.

"Of course you can . . ." I said.

"When you say that writing's like life, do you mean you write stories about things that in some way or another have happened to you, is that it?"

"Yes."

"So if you want your hero to be in love, it has to be the same in your life. I mean, you have to be in love yourself, right?"

"Yes, that makes sense."

"It's not stupid?"

"No. In fact, it's something I knew and I even wanted to put into practice . . ."

"I see . . . So why don't you?"

"No idea," I said rather curtly. She gave me a shifty look.

"Are you mad at me?"

"Of course not," I said.

No, I can admit it: I was a little irritated at being caught out by La Petite. Besides that, the combination of white wine, peanut butter, and strawberry jam was making me feel sick.

To settle my stomach, I decided to make some real coffee. I went to the cupboard and took out the old coffeepot I never use anymore because filters are simpler to use. When the aroma of freshly brewed coffee filled the kitchen, La Petite brought me cups, milk, and sugar.

"That smells good!" she said.

"Want a cup?" I asked.

"Please," she said in her little voice.

After pouring the coffee, I stood there leaning on the counter, looking out the window at the river, and I began to think about Marika. I was thinking about her with all my soul and with all my might. During these last weeks, my attitude toward her hadn't been proper. Not that I'd forgotten her – she still had a place in my heart – but I hadn't taken care of her as well as I should have.

She had arrived in my life at exactly the right time: during a period when I was trying to write a love story. She was a gift from the gods. A mysterious woman, near yet remote, practical and dreamy; she had a sense of reality and a romantic spirit; like me, she was a loner, but she was beautiful too, and a kind of sensuality radiated from the objects with which she surrounded herself.

Besides, I knew from what my brother had told me, and from my own observations one foggy night, that there was a bizarre resemblance between us.

And what had my attitude been? That of a man who is intrigued, perturbed, who feels an attraction mingled with fear. I had gone to look in the cave several times but without attaching any particular importance, hurriedly, quite prepared to be satisfied with what others – La Petite, Bungalow, my brother – could tell me about her . . . And for some weeks now, on the pretext that we could use the mailbox to communicate, I'd made no more effort to see her, taking convenient refuge in my story.

It was a reaction of fear.

"Are you thinking about Marika?" asked La Petite.

No, indeed, you couldn't hide anything from her.

"Yes," I said, "but how did you know?"

"I can guess what's going on in people's minds," she said. "In my mind, everything's all mixed up, and I can't make heads or tails of it, but with other people I can see clearly what's going on."

"It's the same with me," I said, taking a sip of coffee.

In spite of the difference in age and the other differences, which were many, La Petite and I had several things in common. And the most important of those common points, at least the one that brought me closest to her, was perhaps this: most of the time we were, both of us, walled up inside ourselves and busy trying to stick back together the fragments of our past.

AUTUMN LIGHT

The light was different now.

I had just arrived on the beach, and I was walking toward the cave, my heart filled with Marika's presence, when all at once I became aware of it: the air was clear, you could see far away into the distance, the beautiful autumn light was here.

I stopped for a moment to take a better look. The sky was a deeper shade of blue. The metal framework of the two bridges stood out more clearly against the horizon. Across the river, the white patches of houses lost in the greenery on the side of the cliff were more dazzling.

As I brought my gaze back to the shore, I suddenly noticed that the white flag on the mailbox had been lifted. It was very far away, at the limit of my field of vision, but I could clearly see the white square standing out against the slate gray of the cliff; there was a message! I started to run, and when I was just ten meters from the mailbox, out of breath, the white flag . . . suddenly, to my amazement, flew away! I'd made a mistake. It was a gull!

I started walking toward the cave, shamefaced and irritated at my error. How could I have confused a seagull with a white flag? How could anyone be such a fool? Good thing nobody'd seen me! . . . I tried to recover from this self-loathing and regain the self-confidence I'd had half an hour earlier, after I had shaved, showered, washed my hair, and discreetly dabbed on some cologne before I left the house to go and see Marika.

It was Saturday morning. I'd spent a restless night, tossing and turning in my bed, prey to some ancient and primitive fears that had so tormented me when I was little: a fear of falling into the void, of being devoured by wolves . . . things like that.

Why had these old fears (as old as I or, perhaps I should say, as old as humanity) suddenly come back to plague me? I had sat up in my bed, trying to ponder this question, but I hadn't found a satisfactory answer: serious thinking doesn't come easily to me – I was more accustomed to dreaming or daydreaming, allowing things to be untangled by themselves.

But now as I walked along the beach, already crossing the scree, I experienced no fear. I felt calm, lighthearted, and comfortably wrapped in my soul. Unlike what had happened on previous visits, my courage did not falter even briefly when I saw that the sailboat was anchored across from the cave, and the little skiff tied to the stake on the beach. I was even glad to know Marika was home, and it seemed to me that this time everything was going to proceed very simply. After making a little noise to warn her, I was going to step inside the cave saying, Hello, I'm your neighbor, my name is Jim . . . She would shake my hand, saying, I'm Marika, I really enjoyed that text by Paul Hazard you left for me the other day, I'd intended to go to your house and thank you but unfortunately I was very caught up with my work on the sailboat . . . I'd tell her I understood perfectly, and she would smile very sweetly as she said, I've just made some coffee on my little Coleman stove, would you like a cup?

I noticed that the sailboat had been repainted blue and white and no longer listed to one side. When I got to the cave, I called out vigorously: "Yoo-hoo! Anybody home?" and went in without waiting for an answer. I had mentally prepared a little phrase I would offer by way of greeting, but I didn't get the chance to use it: no one was there. I looked in both rooms. There really was no one home.

And yet everything was still in place: in the back room, the sleeping back with its fragrance of clover, and the toilet kit; in the big room, the load of firewood, the Coleman stove and the lamp, the rest of the camping equipment and the groceries, and the copy of *The Arabian Nights* on the rocky ledge. When I looked at the book, I was amazed to see that the bookmark now was almost at the end. Marika had read a lot since my last visit. She'd read the seven "Voyages of Sinbad the Sailor" and two other stories, including "Aladdin or the Wonderful Lamp," and now she was at the "Tale of Ali Baba and the Forty

Thieves Exterminated by a Slave." With a pang, I saw in the table of contents that after Ali Baba there were only three stories left, fairly short ones at that.

A vague threat hovered over me. It was a sensation like the one I'd felt the week before my wife ran away with Superman. I began to walk through the cave, looking all around, and for the first time I realized that there was no object, no article of clothing for instance, that would have been proof positive of a woman's presence. In short, there was nothing but the name on the flyleaf of *The Arabian Nights*. And on the sand, a multitude of bare footprints exactly the size of my own.

As I was leaving the cave it occurred to me that Marika might be out on her sailboat. After a brief hesitation, which I overcame by thinking about Hemingway, I pulled off my T-shirt, my jeans, and my old running shoes, and went into the water. The sailboat was only fifty meters from shore so I was sure I could walk to it, but the bottom dropped off suddenly and, having lost my footing, I was forced to swim. I'm a very poor swimmer and water is a hostile element for me. If I were obliged to swim with just one arm, holding aloft a bottle of champagne and two glasses in the other hand, with my clothes tied around my head, I most certainly would have drowned . . . But conditions were favorable: the ebbing tide was pulling me toward the sailboat so that a few awkward breaststrokes brought me to it, and by gripping the mooring cable, I was able to hoist myself onboard.

Under my weight the little sailboat had listed slightly, and any moment now Marika would surely open the hatch cover to investigate what was going on. While I waited for her to appear, I sat on the deck, wearing just my underwear, shivering because I was wet. I waited for a few minutes, tense, my heart pounding, and then it occurred to me that she might be sleeping. To wake her gently I started singing the Brassens song that's always in my head; the words are by Aragon and it's one of my very favorite songs. I sang two verses, then I pricked up my ears: not a sound. I asked out loud if anyone was there. After listening in vain for a reply, I knocked on the hatch three times and went down the ladder. I had to bow to the evidence: no one was there.

Marika's sailboat was small, but it had been fixed up cozily and tastefully. In addition to the navigational instruments, there were a bunk, a foldaway table, a small bookcase, a kitchen nook, and blue curtains at the windows. Everything was clean and freshly painted.

As I had done in the cave, I looked all around for signs of a female presence, but I didn't see anything special. My attention was drawn to a big book lying flat in the bookcase. I was attracted to its orange cover, on which I could see as I came closer palm trees, a parrot, and a sun. The book was entitled *Taking Off* and the author, whose name I didn't recognize, was Jacques Massacrier. When I picked up the book, I noticed that it had the appealing subtitle *A Manual of Roaming Under Sail*, so I brought it to the table for a closer look. This time, I was in no hurry. I wasn't paying a hasty little visit. Needless to say, I felt uneasy, and as indiscreet as I'd felt the very first time I'd visited the cave, but I was determined not to leave until I'd seen Marika. Even if you're a Libra, there are times when you must be able to make a decision. I studied the book as calmly as I could, while remaining alert for any sound that might indicate that someone was approaching the sailboat.

The watermark on the book's orange cover was a whole list of nouns having to do with sailing; many were unfamiliar, and I started reading aloud for the pleasure of hearing the sound of the words: *stanchion, windlass, fairlead, blunderbuss, turnbuckle* . . . After that, I opened the book and read the first page, which was lovely and spellbinding:

> *And so, if you would allow yourself to be gently lulled by the waves, you first must leave these high latitudes of ours. Make your way to other, more hospitable seas, where life on the water is good, urged on by kindly winds. All those seas dotted with sublime islands between which crisscross wandering sailors, eaters of horizons who gorge themselves and intoxicate themselves on these ultimate and immense open spaces . . .*

In the galley of Marika's little sailboat, I let myself be lulled by the spell of the words. Time was passing, and I wasn't aware of it, but suddenly I felt a slight pang in my stomach. I looked at my watch: two o'clock. La Petite was probably worrying about my absence. I replaced the book in the bookcase and left.

The tide had gone out and it was very easy to regain the shore on foot. I donned my clothes again and slowly went back to the house, turning several times to see if Marika was anywhere around, but there was no sign of her presence on the beach or on the sandbar or on the water.

A DREAM OF LOVE

One night I had a wonderful dream.

First there was a hazy image: a white-walled room with filtered light and a faint scent of talcum powder. And in the middle of the room, a big bed in which I was lying all alone.

Then the image grew clearer and I began to see colors. The walls, which had seemed at first to be white, now were papered with a design of blue or violet flowers, and the curtains were dark blue. Close to the window sat a pretty dressing table and a three-paneled mirror, and my mother was there, wearing a nightgown and sitting on a stool, her triple face looking out but not seeing me. In front of her were aligned, by order of size, a series of bottles filled with perfumes, creams, and ointments. There was also a jewelry box and a music box that played "Autumn Leaves."

Abruptly, the setting changed. I was still lying in the big bed, but my mother had disappeared and the room was no longer the same: now it was a modern bedroom with pale blue bare plaster walls, a floor of polished oak, and a broad window through which I could hear bird songs and the murmur of a river. With the blankets pulled up to my chin, I watched the gray light of dawn slip slowly into the room. I had never seen this place before, everything in the room was strange to me, but I wasn't surprised to be there: perhaps that was because of the river, which sounded so familiar.

Then all at once I hear another sound: the creaking of a door. Someone has come into the house, and although I'm still lying in the bed, I can *see* what that person is doing: opening the fridge, taking out a tin of chicken and feeding some to the cat, tapping the fork against the rim of the can, dropping the fork in the sink. I can see each one of these acts, but I cannot make out the face; I don't even know if it's a man or a woman. All that I can see quite distinctly are two bare feet.

The person walks onto the staircase that goes up to the second floor. I can see the bare feet climbing the steps one by one. At the top, the person enters the hallway, at the end of which is the bedroom, but there is something peculiar: another staircase. Each time the person arrives at the top of a staircase, there is another one; it's as if time is stretching out to infinity . . .

Once again, the image is transformed. Instead of a bedroom, I am lying now in my old van, in which the backseat has been pulled down to form a bed. It is a real double bed, very comfortable, with sheets and blankets, and the drawn curtains that filter the morning light make it feel like a little house. It is probably in the country: I hear something like a rustle of bare feet in the grass. Sitting up in the bed, I listen carefully. The footsteps are very close and soon the van door opens. My heart stops: it is Marika! . . . I recognize at once the thin bony face that I had glimpsed in the fog the other night. She is wearing very pale blue jeans and a white shirt with the sleeves rolled up, and her feet are bare.

She closes the door gently and glances at the bed. I pretend to be sleeping, but through my half-closed eyelids I see her stand a little to one side, pull off her shirt and drop it onto the passenger seat, then she takes off her jeans and the rest of her clothes. I close my eyes just as she turns to me with a timid smile. I guess that she is quickly approaching the bed, that she is lifting the blankets, and I shift slightly to leave her a warm place.

Now it's as if time has stopped. I don't know what country the old Volks is in, but there must be another river because I can hear murmuring water. Marika is lying against me, on my left. Her head is on my shoulder, my left arm is around her neck, my right one around her waist. I can feel her warm breath on my neck and all the warmth of her body against mine; her feet are a little cold.

I like the roundness of her hips and I very much like the gentle warmth of her belly. I don't know that we can ever feel better than we do at this moment. Of course we could caress one another, make love, try to join together, to become one. Then we could talk, recount, explain . . . We could very well do that, but we wouldn't feel any better than we do now. It's now that we feel best, it's now that we are happy.

EARTHLY PARADISE

What is happiness? An illusion, a dream to be pursued throughout a lifetime . . . one that at certain moments we believe we've attained. It happened to me one day in Venice.

When I was visiting some of the European cities whose names I knew from songs, like thousands before me I had succumbed to the lure of Venice: the water shimmering under her bridges, the sound of footsteps in the little side streets, the cats dozing in public squares, everything created an atmosphere of mystery and melancholy that had cast a spell over me.

I was particularly attached to a little square that for me represented beauty, perfection, earthly paradise. It was chance that had brought me to this place.

Every morning I left the Volks – which was already old and falling apart – in a campground at Mestre, near the airport, and took a bus that dropped me at the train station; from there, on a vaporetto or on foot, depending on my mood and the weather, I would go to the Piazza San Marco, where I liked just strolling around, for the square, perhaps because of its harmonious proportions, gave me a feeling of well-being and security. Then I would leave the square with its hordes of tourists to lose myself in the labyrinth of outlying little streets.

That morning, I came close to being really lost. I'd probably gone in a circle because I crossed over the Rialto twice and then, it seemed to me, I walked east, past the church of San Giovanni e Paolo, then I turned south just before the Arsenale. And it was probably near there that all at once, when I emerged from one of the little streets, I walked into the wonderful little square.

Before me was a canal like hundreds of others in Venice, but somewhat narrower than most; it was straddled by an elegantly curved little bridge with a parapet just low enough to invite you to sit down; it was surrounded by brick houses that were beige, almost caramel in color, their windows adorned with red and white flowers and with yellow plastic weather vanes; finally, to liven up the scene, just next to it there was a *bar-tabac*, its windows full of trinkets.

When I found the little square, it was deserted, and since I was tired and a little absentminded, I didn't notice that it was lovely too. (I say that rather sadly: most of the time we see almost nothing.) However, I could sense, I could guess that something was going to happen when I sat in a sunny corner with my back against the old stones. My soul was soft and warm around me. I started watching very attentively.

After a few minutes, I saw that there was a felicitous blend of light and shadow; that the shuddering water in the canal, when it reflected the light, broke it into a thousand fragments that streamed under the arch of the bridge and up the faded brick wall; that the colors were soothing to the eye, with some brighter patches here and there, and that all the shapes that made up the setting of this little square were in harmony with one another. In a sense it was perfection, earthly paradise, as if an old dream had materialized, and I stayed there, sitting in my corner, moved and overcome by admiration, until the end of the day.

The next day, as soon as I woke up in the Mestre campground, I felt a compelling urge to return to my anonymous little square. Again, I took the bus into Venice, then I walked to the Rialto and from there, heading toward the Arsenale, I tried to follow the same route I had taken the day before. In vain, I wandered the streets all that day and the next, but I was unable to find again the little square that had appeared to me like paradise . . . And today I don't even know if it really exists.

A FIRE ON THE BEACH

Was it wiser to seek happiness within oneself? While I wasn't altogether sure, I had good reason to think so, because of a certain number of changes that had occurred in me since my dream of love.

After that dream, in fact, I was no longer the same. The image of Marika was within me, settled there permanently, and whenever I thought of her, I felt a sensation of warmth in my chest, on the left side, as if my heart had begun to melt. I was in love.

With no effort, I could summon up not only her angular face, her eyes that almost shut when she smiled, and her black, curly hair that was starting to go gray, but also her narrow shoulders, her slender body, her hands and feet, which were, strangely, the same length as mine.

And besides, my senses became keener. I shuddered when La Petite

or Bungalow, walking past me in the house, grazed my elbow . . .
I rediscovered all kinds of old smells, especially in my parents' bedroom . . . On the beach, the odor of sea wrack seemed stronger than
usual . . . I could distinguish colors better: the discrete shades of green
in the trees' foliage, the blue of the sky, which was dark above my head
and paler on the horizon, the silvery sparkle of light on the river, the
bright spots scattered here and there by clothing, flowers, gulls, boats,
the roofs of houses.

I was at once happy and unhappy. It was sweet and comforting to
know that Marika was nearby, that whenever I wanted to, I could go
and warm my heart at that immense source of heat. And I took satisfaction from the fact that part of me, which I'd thought to be numb
forever because of my age, had suddenly wakened and was giving
me a new desire to live. At the same time, though, I was worried.
I was afraid that my whole life was going to change. I was afraid of
losing not my freedom, but rather my leisure activities, in particular
my idleness, my eternal idleness that served no useful purpose but
accomplished everything.

What was oddest was that, for no apparent reason, I was often on
the verge of tears. La Petite thought I was weird . . . One night when
we'd made a fire on the shore because it had turned chilly, she wanted
to know if everything was all right.

"Have you got smoke in your eyes?" she asked.

"A little," I said.

We were on either side of the fire, with me sitting on a rock and she
on an old tree trunk, each of us wrapped in a woolen blanket. We'd

made a good fire from twigs, birch bark, dead branches, and several logs that had gotten away from the boats; it was burning well, but it was a little smoky because of the seaweed.

"You can come and sit here," she said.

"All right," I said, wiping my eyes.

Like me, La Petite was no longer quite the same. There was something very mysterious about her now. She had just located her real family (Bungalow had told me on the phone), but she hadn't yet said anything about it.

"Is that better?" she asked when I was sitting on the tree trunk beside her.

"Much better," I said. "Are you all right?"

"Yes and no."

"We haven't seen much of each other today . . . Did you do anything special?"

"I thought."

"Oh, yes?"

I didn't dare ply her with questions, not knowing whether she felt like talking about what had happened. She rose, picked up a long branch, and slowly raked up the coals that were scattered around the fire. Then she made her decision:

"I've found my real parents, but . . . it wasn't exactly the way I pictured it."

She came back and sat on the tree trunk, staring silently at the glowing embers. Then, as gently as I could, I asked:

"What was it that you'd pictured?"

"Oh, well . . . I'd imagined they'd act the way people do when you've lost . . . when you've lost something very precious and then all of a sudden, when you'd almost forgotten it existed, you find it by chance . . . I'd imagined them with shining eyes and a kind of light in their faces."

"And it wasn't like that?"

"No. When I got there it was suppertime. There was just my father and my mother, no children. And I came by myself. I saw them through the window when I got there: they were in the kitchen, eating and watching TV, I rang the bell . . ."

La Petite stopped talking, or, more precisely, her voice, which was already tiny and fragile, broke. I was hanging on her every word. I held my breath and I think that the river just beside us, the old river that for three and a half centuries had been listening to the secrets of an entire nation, was holding its breath as well.

She shuddered, hugged herself in her blanket, then began again:

"He opened the door and looked me up and down . . . the way men look at women, you know?"

"Yes," I murmured. "And then what?"

"I saw that our eyes and mouths were almost the same, but he didn't notice, he just asked what I wanted. I told him I wanted a glass of water. He went back to his . . . to my mother and he said: 'It's a girl that wants a glass of water.' My mother said: 'Fine, give her one.' She only glanced at me when I went into the kitchen. She went on eating and watching TV."

She stopped.

"And then?" I said.

"That's all," she said. "I drank the water and left."

She was silent and this time I didn't wait, I wrapped my blanket around her shoulders on top of hers. All her life she had been pursuing a dream, and just as she thought she'd attained it, it had vanished. I wanted to show her that there were still reasons to hope, that there was still some warmth in this rotten world; if I could have, I swear I'd have placed her under the protection of my soul, the better to warm her and keep her safe from human aggressiveness.

She huddled against me and cried for a while, but not for very long, I mean not as long as I would have expected. I was amazed, really, to see how strong she was despite appearances. Finally she sniffed, blew her nose loudly in an old Kleenex, then started asking me questions the way she often did. She asked if I'd gone back to writing.

"Not yet," I said, "but I will soon."

"How do you know?" she asked.

"For the past few days it's been moving inside me: there's something coming."

"Will you be going back to the same story?"

"No, I think I'll be starting a new one."

"Another love story?"

"Of course!"

La Petite was observing me through her lock of hair. It was now or never if I was going to tell her I was in love, but I couldn't do it. Perhaps it was too personal, too intimate, like a kind of secret. Or perhaps I just simply couldn't explain that I was in love with a person whom I'd never seen, except in a dream . . . In a voice that was still broken by a little sadness, she asked:

"Besides your writing, is there anything that matters to you a lot?"

I tried to think . . . First of all I thought about tennis, but then I remembered that for five years, following my back injury, I hadn't played at all, and the inactivity hadn't been all that painful . . . Then I thought about friendship, but I immediately remembered that when I was traveling in Europe I hadn't once felt the need to send my friends a letter or even a postcard . . .

"I don't think so," I said finally.

"And why do you write books?" she asked.

"I'd like to write the most beautiful story that has ever been written. But it's hard, it's really too hard for me, it's impossible, so every time I have to start all over."

"You aren't discouraged?"

"No, but . . ."

No sooner had I said the word than I regretted that "but" I'd left hanging. Now I had to explain myself. I already knew that I was going to say all kinds of nonsense: whenever anyone asked about my work, I had a tendency to exaggerate, to speak without thinking; it was as if someone else was talking in my place.

"*But* . . . but what?" she insisted.

"I'm going to let you in on a secret," I said. "Promise not to tell anybody?"

"Cross my heart!" she said.

In spite of myself, my voice took on a slightly solemn tone.

"Very well," I said, "here goes! . . . Books contain nothing or almost nothing that's important: everything is in the mind of the person reading them."

If you were trying to find an idiotic remark, that one took the cake! La Petite shrank away from me, and I could see by the light of the fire that she was looking at me with eyes widened in surprise.

"Are you pulling my leg?" she asked.

"Absolutely not!" I said.

I sank deeper into my stupidity and didn't know what I could cling to when she started to say:

"Anyway, in your books . . ."

"Yes . . . ?" I said, trying not to show my interest. "I didn't know you read my books."

"In your books," she began again, "I'm sure there must be some important things."

"You think so?"

I didn't want it to show, but I desperately wanted her to explain what she'd just said. Even though writing had been my occupation for more than twenty years, even though I'd written half a dozen books, I was still as sensitive and vulnerable as I'd been at the beginning to the slightest remark about my work.

"I'm sure of it," she replied.

I'd exhausted my "You think so's?" and "Oh yesses?" and I didn't know what I could say to encourage her to tell me exactly what she saw in my books. So I didn't say anything and in no time she'd launched into an explanation on her own.

"I'm a person," she told me, "who always wants to bite. I'm like an alley cat that everybody's mistreated: my normal reaction is to want to bite and scratch. But when I read your books, it's as if I've been given permission to be not so aggressive, to be gentle for a little while. As if somebody had told me: Be gentle if you want, nothing will happen, no one will harm you. Do you understand what I'm trying to say?"

"I understand," I said, as humbly as I could.

"So there's something important in your books," she concluded. "That makes sense, doesn't it?"

"Sounds like it to me . . ."

I did my best to conceal my satisfaction. Actually, I was flattered and absolutely delighted at what she'd said. This girl was no literary expert, she didn't write articles for *Le Devoir* or *Le Monde* or the *New York Times*, but as far as aggressiveness and the need for affection were concerned, she had plenty of experience.

It wouldn't have taken much for me to tell her another secret, one I hadn't dared to share with anyone yet: in spite of my infantile fears, I harbored a naive and disproportionate ambition to contribute, through my writing, to the advent of a new world, a world where there would be no violence, no wars between nations, no quarrels between individuals, no competition or rivalry in the workplace, a world where aggressiveness – understood not as an expression of hostility toward others but as an appetite for life – would be at the service of love.

I kept that huge and foolish secret to myself. In any case, there was an urgent, concrete problem: La Petite was hungry. I went to the house for some bread and butter, then I made toast on the coals, went back to the house again to make hot chocolate, then one last time to get a big bag of marshmallows, which she roasted on the end of a stick. Later, she lay down on the sand beside an old tree trunk and fell asleep, muffled to the eyes in her blanket. She slept soundly and I stayed beside her until morning, maintaining the fire so she wouldn't catch cold, because the night was chilly and damp.

At daybreak, old Mr. Blue came looking for me and he sat in my lap and purred for a while. To pass the time, I looked at the stars or at the boats whose green or red lights were gliding along the water. I kept an eye on the tide as it came in. In a corner of my heart, like a glowing lamp, there was also the thought that Marika was very close to me.

THE PHANTOM VESSEL

By late September, the cool air gave way to an unexpected heat wave that could only be short-lived: Indian summer. Once again, there were fog banks on the river.

One day when I had worked a lot despite the heat, I had an urge to seek a little coolness on the water; late that afternoon I got the old emergency raft from the shed.

It wasn't a simple polyethylene raft like the ones you see floating in a swimming pool or that you rent for sunbathing during a seaside vacation. It was a real U.S. Navy rescue raft, as indicated by the inscription "U.S. Navy" in black letters on its outer flank. Made of bright yellow rubber, very thick and resistant, it was equipped with two oars and a waterproof chest that held emergency flares, packets of dehydrated food, and everything you'd need to survive a shipwreck.

My father had bought it secondhand from Latulippe War Surplus, and the salesman had told him that it may have shot the rapids of the Colorado River, which runs through the Grand Canyon. Actually, I don't remember if the salesman really said that it had shot the Colorado rapids or just that it was tough enough to have done so; whatever the case may be, everyone agreed that there was no better rescue craft available.

It wasn't used often, and I remembered why when I started taking it from the shed: the raft was very heavy. Fortunately, the tide was in, and I didn't have too much trouble dragging it onto the sloping beach and to the water's edge. Before I set out, though, I'd have to inflate it with a foot pump. It wasn't completely deflated: it only lacked the amount of air that had been removed for storage, but because of the oppressive heat, it took all my energy to pump it up, and I barely had the strength to give the raft a push before I collapsed inside it.

Exhausted and out of breath, for a long time I just lay there on my back. The sky was veiled by layers of fog that gave occasional glimpses of the sun, which was as red as a fireball. I was drenched with sweat, and since there wasn't a breath of wind and the tide was slack, there was no risk of drifting away, so I took off my wet clothes and closed my eyes.

Did the heat and my fatigue put me to sleep for a while? I think they did, because when I opened my eyes and sat up, I realized that I could no longer see the house or even the shoreline. By temperament I'm inclined to get nervous under such circumstances, but this time I stayed absolutely calm, knowing very well that there was a compass in the waterproof chest, and that a few strokes of the oars would take me back to shore.

However, I made two observations: the fog was slightly thicker now, and little waves were lapping at the walls of the raft. I was beginning to wonder if the tide, as it began to ebb, had taken me out to the middle of the river . . . I stuck my hand in the water to determine if there was a current, but I didn't feel any. Then I leaned overboard to assess the water's depth; you couldn't see anything, the water was gray and dirty.

My head and shoulders were still outside the raft when all at once a heavy swell lifted it up and pushed me over backward. When I heard the muffled roar of a siren far away on the river, I realized that a ship of heavy tonnage had just gone out to sea, and I sat there in the raft, naked, laughing at my misfortune, and waiting for the second swell. After this one, which was not as heavy as the first, had lifted the raft, I opened the chest, took out the compass, oriented myself, and settled in at the oars.

After I'd rowed with all my might for five or ten minutes, I started to worry because the shoreline still wasn't in view. My nervousness growing, I turned my head after every stroke of the oars and tried to spot the shoreline or some reference point. And suddenly I had a sort of vision.

I had just turned my head when all at once, through a clearing in the fog, I saw, or thought I saw, Marika's sailboat gliding through the water like a phantom vessel. It lasted only one brief moment, but before my eyes was the freshly painted little sailboat, its mainsail folded. I couldn't see the name on the hull; that detail was unimportant, however, as the sailboat had appeared to me at an angle, more precisely in three-quarter view from behind.

In any case, it wasn't till later that I paid any attention to the details: for the moment, I was too excited and too afraid of being carried away by the tide, of drifting to the canal, of being overturned by a freighter. But when I was finally back on shore and I'd pulled the raft onto the beach, the vision grew strangely more precise. I saw again very clearly the little blue-and-white sailboat, its sail furled and lashed to the boom as it glided silently through the fog . . . And then I thought: if the sailboat wasn't under sail, it must have a motor, and I hadn't heard a motor. Why?

I tried to find an explanation while I was cooking spaghetti for myself and La Petite. All I could think of, after we'd finished eating, was this: the hum of the little motor had been covered by the sound I was making myself when I plunged my oars in the water. But that explanation wasn't very convincing, and I tried all evening and into the night to find another one.

My attempts led nowhere. They even planted some doubt in my mind. At dawn I still hadn't slept, I kept tossing and turning in my bed, and I didn't even know if I'd really seen Marika's sailboat.

THE FINAL VISIT

At the first light of dawn I woke with a start, and without even taking time to dress, I went up to the attic to see if the sailboat was still across from the sandy inlet. I opened the dormer window and leaned out to look toward the right side of the bay, first with my naked eyes and then with the binoculars, but there were layers of fog that thinned out on the sandbar. I could see practically nothing.

I replaced the binoculars in the desk drawer and once again – I couldn't help myself – I had no choice but to look at what I'd written. The first pages of the new love story were just in front of me on the breadbox. Their peculiar look testified to my attempts to include passages from the old story: they were made up of pieces of paper that had been cut out with scissors and taped together. I suddenly thought of my readers, my poor readers, and wondered what they'd have thought of me if they could have seen that my love story was concocted from such ridiculous means as this cutting and pasting. Perhaps they didn't know that, more often than not, stories are written out of used materials and that it's up to the author to make it all look new.

On my way downstairs to the kitchen, I stopped on the second floor, where the door to my younger brother's bedroom was open. I approached it to see if La Petite was awake. She was still sleeping, not in the little bed with metal bars but in the big bed. Around her were an amazing number of books, among which I recognized some Jules Verne and some old titles from the Signes de Piste series that came from one of the bookcases on the sun porch; the way the books were arranged around her made it look as if she was trying to erect a rampart between herself and the outside world.

Old Mr. Blue was at the foot of the bed. On spying me he jumped to the floor without a sound and followed me to the staircase. In the kitchen I fed him some chicken, then I made coffee and fixed myself some orange juice and cereal. I hadn't downed half of my cornflakes when I had a sudden, irresistible urge to see what was going on in the cave. It's rare that I give in, with no critical judgment, to such an impulse, but that morning the desire rose in me like a groundswell that swept away everything in its wake.

Unable to think, I abandoned my breakfast and left the house without even shutting the door. It took me a moment to realize that I was barefoot. I walked quickly, thinking about Marika. My heart was filled with her, and I was anxious to see her. Now and then I broke into a run. I was short of breath and drenched with sweat, but I felt good: I was in love, my soul was transparent, and my whole body was throbbing with life.

I stopped briefly at the mailbox. It was obvious there was nothing in it: the white flag hadn't been raised, but I went up to it all the same and looked inside, because I needed to catch my breath. I saw that the bottom of the box was covered with twigs and moss, and that reminded me of a little story Gabrielle Roy had told me.

Gabrielle Roy used to spend her summers at Petite-Rivière-Saint-François, along the river, in a cottage that clung to a hillside. It was her habit to step onto the gallery in the morning to brush her hair; before she went back inside she would clean the brush, letting the hair fly away in the wind. She had observed a robin flying back and forth, which seemed to have its nest in a bush at the back of her garden, and she'd become accustomed to its presence. But in September, after the birds had flown south, she'd discovered when she approached the bush that the robin had lined its nest with the hairs she had lost during the summer.

This story didn't come back to me in all its details, only two or three quick images, and I immediately started back toward the cave. I was walking at a good clip. Just past the scree I was expecting to see the little sailboat, but there was some lingering fog, just enough so that I couldn't tell if it was there or not. And then anxiety swept over me, an insane anxiety that made me run straight to the cave, even though I was scraping the soles of my feet on the sharp pebbles.

When I reached the sandy inlet, I had to face up to it: the sailboat was no longer there. This time it wasn't the fog that was concealing it from my eyes, because a slight breeze was blowing from the west and the weather was clearer. If the sailboat had been in its place, pulling on its anchor a few cables' length from the cave, I'd have spotted it at first glance. It was gone.

I tried to reassure myself, saying that this wasn't the first time the sailboat had been absent just when I was coming to see Marika, that there was no reason to panic, but it wasn't enough to calm my anxiety. I felt a foreboding; I could sense that something serious was going to happen.

I took a few steps toward the cave. Then I hesitated. After all, I wasn't obliged to go in, to check. As long as I hadn't gone inside, there was still a chance . . . I finally decided it was better to be clear about it in my own mind, so I ducked my head and slipped in through the breach.

Marika wasn't there, and there was nothing at all in the cave. I looked in both rooms, the living room and the little bedroom, but there was nothing. Not a match, not a scrap of paper, nothing at all. I had a lump in my throat, and my chest was constricted, and my head was as empty as the cave. It was chilly and very damp. I was shivering.

A moment later I came out of the cave and sat on the ground facing the river. The warmth of the air felt good. I was trying to put some order in my thoughts, to comprehend what was happening, when all at once it struck me as absurd that there was really nothing in the cave, not the slightest sign, not even a smell. I slipped back inside and looked all around. Nothing. I sniffed the air in search of the scent I had once detected, in midsummer, that was something like clover, but there really was nothing at all. All that remained finally were the footprints in the sand. The prints of feet that were the same size as mine.

THE ADOPTION

I don't know how much time I spent in the cave and on the beach, asking myself questions to which there were no answers. Probably several hours, because when I returned to the house, exhausted, on the verge of tears and with a growing urge to pour my heart out, La Petite was very worried.

"Where were you?" she snapped the minute I set foot in the kitchen.

I was surprised by her aggressive tone of voice. She wasn't even looking at me: she was holding old Mr. Blue in her arms and looking out the window.

"*Some people* were worried," she said. "*Some people* didn't know what was going on. You didn't finish your cornflakes and the door was wide open . . . *Some people* thought something terrible had happened."

"I went to the cave," I said.

The knot that was constricting my throat was suddenly loosened, and I burst into sobs. I quickly sat down at the table and hid my face in my arms, at once relieved to be able to cry and ashamed to hear the hiccups that were coming from my throat. When I looked up, I was face-to-face with old Mr. Blue, who had jumped onto the table and had stretched out his muzzle toward me to investigate what was going on. Behind him, La Petite was wide-eyed with astonishment.

"What's wrong?" she asked, her voice more gentle now.

"It's Marika," I said. "I went to the cave this morning but she wasn't there. She's gone."

"You know very well she'll be back," she said. "She goes away often, but she always comes back."

"No," I said. "This time she won't come back. The sailboat's gone and the cave is empty. There's nothing left at all."

I was still crying, but the sobbing had stopped. Now it was only tears, and that felt good. The sadness was slowly leaving.

"Don't cry," said La Petite. "Please don't cry."

Her plea was uttered in an authoritarian tone, but I barely noticed: I just wanted to talk, to explain.

"It's my own fault," I said. "I should have known she was leaving . . . I was so busy writing, I didn't pay any attention to the signs."

"What signs?" she asked.

"There was the copy of *The Arabian Nights* that was nearly finished, and the ghost ship in the fog . . ."

"You mustn't cry," she said.

"I'm getting old and I still don't know how to live. It's something I forgot to learn," I said ironically.

"I'm hungry," she said.

Looking at the Coca-Cola clock, I saw that it was almost seven. La Petite probably hadn't eaten since morning: it was perfectly normal for her to be hungry, and my stomach felt empty too.

"What would you like to eat?" I asked.

"Bacon and eggs," she said. "And toast and peanut butter."

I fixed her what she'd asked for. When I was cooking the bacon, I added a few pinches of brown sugar to give it the little hint of sweetness that she liked so much. She sat down across from me and took a big mouthful, washing it down with hot chocolate.

"It's very good," she said. "Thanks a lot, you're really sweet to take such good care of me."

"It's nothing," I said.

"Do you feel better now?" she asked.

"A little," I said.

"Still thinking about Marika?"

"Yes."

"Is it like having a broken heart?"

"Exactly."

She fed a piece of bacon to old Mr. Blue, who had just jumped onto her lap.

"All right, you can tell me anything you want," she said, "but on one condition . . ."

"What's that?"

"Stop crying."

"Why?"

"Because when you cry I'm absolutely lost. Do you know what I mean?"

I didn't really, but I said yes to avoid complicating her life. Then I started to talk about Marika. For once, I let myself go and said whatever came into my mind, and La Petite listened patiently to the very end, even when I told her things she already knew. Deep down I was really talking to myself. Like someone piecing together a puzzle, I was trying to find a meaning in everything that had happened to me during the summer, I mean the footprints, *The Arabian Nights*, the pointlessness (and the futility) of my attempts to see Marika, her appearance and then the appearance of her sailboat in the fog, the dream of love, my writing problems . . .

If I was unable to find the broader significance of all these events, at least I didn't feel so much like crying, and I felt calmer too. And then a question inched its way through the fog in my brain. At first I pushed it away, but it became more and more insistent, and soon I had no choice but to deal with it. I frowned and La Petite noticed.

"What's wrong?" she asked.

"I wonder if Marika really exists," I said.

"What?" she said.

"Perhaps she doesn't exist," I said. "After all, I'm not absolutely sure I saw her."

While I was speaking I didn't take my eyes off La Petite's face. I was waiting for her reaction. I hoped with all my heart that she would protest vigorously, tell me it was a stupid idea because she had seen Marika herself more than once. But instead she lowered her head, and all I could see was the heavy lock of hair falling over her face. When Mr. Blue jumped onto the table again, she let him eat everything that was left on her plate, then she asked:

"But . . . didn't you see her sleeping bag and things in the cave?"

"Yes," I said.

"And the sailboat?"

"Yes."

"Your little brother saw Marika and talked to her?"

"That's what he told me."

It was possible that my brother had invented certain details to please me or to reassure me, but La Petite didn't give me time to set forth this possibility. Some of her usual defiance had come back and she was peppering me with questions like a machine gun.

"And she was the same woman you saw on the night of that famous fog on the river?"

"That's what I thought," I said, "but it's possible I made a mistake."

"But you didn't make a mistake when you saw her name in that copy of *The Arabian Nights*, did you?"

"No, but . . ."

I was going to say that it was no proof, the book could have belonged to someone else, but I was in no mood to argue. Instead, I was trying to understand. And a second thought occurred to me, still vague, one that I couldn't put into words. I felt old and tired. Why was it so hard to find words as I got older?

The second thought became clear only late that evening, under the cover of darkness, as if it were ashamed of itself. To myself, I formulated it more or less like this: Marika didn't really exist, she was merely the projection of a desire, a part of myself, the feminine half, the gentle half.

Secretly, deep down, something about this rather strange idea appealed to me, even pleased me immensely, but it was the kind of idea that sounds ridiculous when you try explaining it to someone else, so I said nothing to La Petite. In any case, she wasn't there. She had gone upstairs to my brother's bedroom, leaving me alone in the kitchen with Mr. Blue.

When I went upstairs to say goodnight, I found her reading, sheltered behind a rampart of books as she'd been the night before. The book that she was reading was *Le Grand Meaulnes*.

"Goodnight," I said, stopping on the threshold.

"Goodnight," she said.

There was fog in her voice, which was even fainter and huskier than usual, and her eyes were rather misty. It was as if she were enveloped in the melancholy of the book she was reading, so I half started to retreat.

"You can come in," she said softly.

She moved some books and beckoned to me to sit at the foot of the bed, and then she sat up, wedging the pillows behind her back. There was something different about her; she seemed older but perhaps that was because of her nightgown. I may be wrong, but I think it was the first time I'd seen her in a nightgown instead of a T-shirt. It was pale blue and it looked familiar; perhaps it had belonged to my sister.

"Did you find what you were looking for?" she asked.

"No," I said, "but it doesn't matter. Sometimes the answers just don't want to come. And sometimes you only come up with questions."

"Are you still upset?"

"A little."

"What are you going to do?"

"What I said: I'm going to try to write the most beautiful love story that's ever been written."

La Petite broke into a smile.

"And those questions you just told me about, will they go into your story?" she asked.

"Certainly," I said.

She tilted her head to one side and her smile was really very sweet. When that tormented and defiant girl turned sweet like that, it was something to see. Suddenly old Mr. Blue came in from the kitchen, followed by the little white cat and her three kittens, who had decided to leave the cellar. They all clambered onto the bed, settled in among the books, and started purring in chorus.

"What about the cats, will you put them in your story too?" she asked, smiling.

"Maybe," I said.

"You should put in some songs and books and a lot of warmth too."

"All right."

"It will be a beautiful story," she said.

"I hope so," I said. "What about you, what are you going to do?"

I'd been wanting to ask her that for a while, but I had never dared.

"Me?" she asked.

"Yes."

"What I'd like to do," she said, "is stay here. I'd like to stay here in this old house. And I'd like . . ."

She was groping for words. She gestured impatiently, then said abruptly:

"Adopt me!"

"Excuse me?" I said.

I wasn't sure I'd heard her correctly.

"Adopt me," she repeated. "I'd like to stay here with you and the animals . . ."

I didn't want her to see, but what she'd just said was completely beyond me, and I was assailed by a host of questions. Would the old house stand up during the winter? Would the oil furnace be enough to heat the house during the January and February cold snaps? How would I clear the snow off the path on the cliff? Would I be able to take care of La Petite, to console her when she was unhappy? Would her presence keep me from writing? Or going out? Or playing tennis?

"Don't you want to?" she asked.

"Of course I want to," I said, with all the determination I could muster.

"Then write it down," she said.

"All right," I said. I looked around the bedroom. There was nothing to write on.

"Let's go to the attic," she said.

I went up the stairs first and La Petite in her blue nightgown followed, while behind her in procession came old Mr. Blue, then the white cat and her three kittens. As I was climbing the stairs, two or three other questions came and badgered me, but at the same time I thought of a solution to the problems of heating and snow clearance. I reminded myself that my father had always lived in the house during the winter, and he had been able to solve all those problems, so I should be able to do the same. Besides, Bungalow could give me a hand with the house and with La Petite.

In the attic, I switched on the desk lamp. La Petite and the cats came and stood all around me while I took from the breadbox a pen and a pad of the graph paper on which I jotted down ideas for my story.

I tried to think of a special wording, something that would seem official, but I couldn't come up with anything satisfactory, so I simply wrote: DEAR PETITE, I ADOPT YOU on a sheet of paper, and at the bottom I put the place, the date, and my signature. La Petite was reading over my shoulder. I folded the paper, put it in the envelope, and handed it to her.

She said simply, "Thank you."

She gestured to us to come with her and, holding the envelope, she went downstairs with the rest of us following, first the cats and then me, to the main floor. She went into the little bedroom and opened the chest with its ornamental gilt hinges. We were all around her when she sealed the envelope and dropped it silently inside the old chest. The cats and I watched her, unmoving and filled with admiration, and I don't know if they were seeing the same thing as I, but the soft, bluish light that illuminated her face turned my heart upside down.